If Looks Could Kill

Jeanne Lazo

To my dear sister, Shelley,
Without you, this would
never have been possible.
Thank you so much.
I love you,
Jeanne
4/17/05

Published by Stargazer Publishing Company
PO Box 77002
Corona, CA 92877-0100
(800) 606-7895
(951) 898-4619
FAX (951) 898-4633
Corporate e-mail: stargazer@stargazerpub.com
Orders by e-mail: orders@stargazerpub.com
www.stargazerpub.com

Edited by Carol J. Amato
Cover illustration by Cristina McAllister

ISBN: 0-9713756-4-X

LCCN: 2004117148

Juvenile Fiction/Mystery

Copyright © 2005 Jeanne Lazo

Printed and bound in the United States of America.

This story contains names of some real places in the towns of Dorseyville and Aspinwall, Pennsylvania. Descriptions, details, and people in the story, however, are fictional.

Dedication

This book is dedicated with loving gratitude to God, from whom all creativity flows; to my sister, Shelley, for spending so many hours helping me create humorous, eccentric characters; to my childhood friends, Debbie, Art, and Ken, who gave me the heart and grist for the story; to my husband, Gene, for believing in me and helping me achieve my dreams; to my dear friend and editor, Carol J. Amato, who taught me how to turn a story into a real book; to my friends at the Writers' Club of Whittier, Inc., Whittier, California, for teaching me the art of writing; to my children, Kim, Rhonda, Larry, Genemar, and Myrrha, and my grandsons, Blake, Spencer, and Parker, for letting me accompany them back to the magical land of childhood; and to my parents, Mary and Buzz Bayne, for giving me the final ingredient I needed to write this story: courage.

The Real Places That Inspired the Story

"Death Tree" in Pine Creek Presbyterian Cemetery,
Dorseyville, PA

J & W Variety Store & US Post Office, Aspinwall, PA

Brilliant Market, Aspinwall, PA

*Many thanks to those who gave the author permission to
use the names of real places and these photos!*

Chapter 1: Wrong Place, Wrong Time

"Priggggs...come here, Priggs. I want to bite you!" Art sounded like a cartoon Dracula as moonlight tap-danced over his wind-swept black cape with its fiery-red lining.

I couldn't decide whether to bite him or kiss him. Did I say kiss? I meant kick. Not in my lifetime, even for a million dollars, would I kiss him.

Fourteen might be too old for trick-or-treating in some towns but not in The Village of Dorseyville. Dorseyville, lies northeast of Pittsburgh, Pennsylvania, off Route 910, a road that probably leads to Somewhere, which must be a town about a million miles from here. In these wooded hills, too remote for streetlights or side-walks, where our neighbors were a bullhorn blast away, we did what we could for fun. "We" included me, Priggs (short for Priscilla Griggs), Fawn Flodi, my best friend, and our closest neighbors, Art Zampini and Tucker Riggoli.

1

Art ran on ahead, making his way through the trees that bordered the Pine Creek Presbyterian Cemetery. "Let's look for Captain Bridgeway's headstone," he hollered.

"No way!" I shouted. "We're not going anywhere near that cemetery tonight!" I spoke for myself as well as Tucker and Fawn. I had no choice but to speak for them; Tucker spoke only in whispers, and Fawn's runway model costume gripped her legs so tightly she could hardly keep up. Through the trees, I could see Art's cape flapping. Already he was swooping past a row of skeleton calling cards made of granite.

"We have to find it for our report—why not now?" he called over his shoulder.

"Absolutely not!" I adjusted the light on my coal miner's hat. "Did you hear me, Pini?" Art hated being called "Pini," but I couldn't resist teasing him, especially tonight, when he was doing his best to annoy me.

Rushing winds snaked through the trees. It was obvious Art hadn't heard me, forcing me to set foot on the hallowed grounds of the cemetery to make my point. "We are *not* going headstone hunting tonight!" I stopped to roll up the cuffs on my jacket. "I don't know why Fawn and I agreed to go Halloweening with you and Tucker at all. Don't press your luck."

"Yeah," Fawn said, but not loud enough for Art to hear.

Ignoring us, Art swished further away from us, shining the light from his flashlight over another row of headstones. Made of black slate or white sandstone, they were thin and brittle with parts of the names worn away. Campbells, McClellands, Crawfords…the weathered markers read like a "Who's Who of Scottish Settlers"— the descendents of the original Scotsmen who had been given land grants in this area for serving in the Revolutionary War. I wondered why kids hadn't stolen the headstones to use as Halloween decorations in their yards; they were that perfect.

The wind whipped through the hills, catching my unzipped coat, blasting my middle with cold air. A second gust roared past my ears as though the Captain himself were shouting to me. I shivered with the cold and the heebie-jeebies.

A dead body hadn't disturbed this ground for more than a hundred years. Although surrounded by dense forests, only one oak had dared to set down roots in the cemetery. It had grown tall; grown, that is, until the first body had been laid to rest. That's when it had been struck dead, its top ripped off, as if by some giant's hand. Thereafter, the locals had called it the Death Tree. The hollow trunk remained, twisted, its crusty bark covered with petrified tendrils of shriveled vines. Years of wind had carved small holes in places, making it look like a tree house for goblins.

I heard Fawn cry out, "*Ouch!* My gown's caught on a jagger bush." Her sense of style was proving hazardous tonight. Oh, she had listened politely to my warnings about the uneven ground and the cold weather but still insisted on wearing her original creation. The down jacket her mother had carefully wrapped around her shoulders was waiting for her under the neighbor's hedges. I smiled to myself. *I should have known she wouldn't wear it. She loves fashion as much as I love books. She would no more cover her costume than I would burn* Romeo and Juliet. *Stubbornness is such a curse.*

The damp, unsettled earth squished under my hiking boots and gave off a mossy smell as I backtracked to give her a hand. She flipped back her chestnut, elbow-length hair and made another attempt to untangle her dress. I tipped my hat, aiming the miner's light on Fawn's hands to make the job easier.

"Oooo-OOOO-oooo," Art crooned.

"Give it up, Art!" I yelled. "Honestly, you can be such a pain!"

"Do you see the flying bats?" he asked, throwing arcs of light into the night sky in the shape of figure eights.

Tucker's cereal box whistled, sending chills up my spine. I'd been secretly pleased the day he asked me to paint his costume, although I'd pretended otherwise. It wasn't until he pleaded with me and said I was the most talented artist in our class that I agreed to do it. Although the design turned out okay, we should have given more thought to the weather. Gusting winds were threatening to lift him and his costume off the ground. 'No bigger than a cake of soap,' as my grandmother used to say; he needed weights in his shoes tonight.

Normally, Tucker was stuffed into an even bigger box than his Halloween costume—the one his parents put him in. In kindergarten, Tucker came to school on picture-taking day wearing a bow tie. That noose around his neck proved he had passed the first tollbooth on the road to success envisioned by his parents. Kids never forgot the bow tie. It wasn't the only thing that set him apart, however. Unlike the rest of us who came into the world with a clean slate, Tucker was born with a book of rules. Kids weren't eager to make friends with someone tied up so tight inside and out. Except for a constant lip biting habit, Tucker seemed not to notice.

Art had been Tucker's friend for as long as I could remember. It was an odd friendship because they were almost complete opposites. Art was funny and outgoing, while Tucker was practically invisible.

Art's light hovered over the Death Tree.

"IIIIIEEEEEE!" Tucker squealed.

A rush of air circled my neck like an icy scarf.

Art moved the beam to where his Tucker's finger pointed. Sticking out of the hollow trunk of the Death Tree was a ghastly pair of white legs and feet fitted with red, glittering, high-heeled shoes, toes pointing up to the dark heavens.

A joke...a Halloween joke, I thought as Fawn and I stopped walking.

Art laughed. "Somebody stuffed a mannequin in there to scare people. Look at the fake legs."

I relaxed a little at that. Yes, it did look like a prank. I turned my head, shining the light from my helmet into the cavity of the tree. The mangled, swollen face of a woman grinned back at me.

Fawn fainted.

I knew in that instant the woman was real—real and dead.

Chapter 2: Help!

"Run, Tucker! Run! Go to the McKinney's. Call 9-1-1," Art yelled, passing Tucker his flashlight. Tucker took off running with the speed of a hawk-chased chicken, his cereal box swaying from side to side.

I covered my face with my hands. Fear squeezed my chest. Only Art's voice kept me from screaming.

"Priggs, help me!" he called.

"She's de-de-dead," I stammered.

"No, Fawn's not dead," he said as he stooped to check on her. "She just fainted."

"I didn't faint," Fawn said softly. She sat up and adjusted her costume cleavage. "I tripped."

6

"*God.*" It came out of me like a prayer. Reluctantly, I lowered my hands from my face.

"*Priggs, let's get out of here!*" Fawn grabbed my arm. "*Let's go to the McKinney's—now!*"

"Come on, Art! Come with us," I pleaded. I couldn't leave him here alone in the dark. "It's safer if we stay together."

"We should wait for the police," he replied. "Let's wait by the road." His voice had a high-pitched squeak like it did last year.

"What if someone else has been murdered?" I asked. "Do you think there are any more dead bodies here?"

"Yeah, lots of them. Six feet under." Art gave me a push to get me moving in what I hoped was the right direction.

Officer Grady stood with his feet solidly planted beside the O'Hara Township squad car, looking intently at Art, then down at his clipboard. He was a round man with a meaty, firm build. Everything about his body language said, "Don't get in my way."

"So, you say you were in the cemetery looking for Captain Bridgeway's headstone?"

"Yes, sir," Art replied with a military snap in his voice.

"Why tonight? Wouldn't it be easier to look for a headstone in the daylight?" Officer Grady's words were carefully balanced and his eyes were sharp, like those of an eagle, taking in every detail. He shifted his weight as he studied Art's face.

Art cleared his throat. "We were walking by the cemetery to go trick-or-treating, and I thought since we were already—"

"Is that right?" Grady turned to me and asked.

His eyes pierced mine in the same way the revolving red light did on the top of the car roof. I forced my eyes to focus on his, so they wouldn't follow the light as it rotated around the trees, the headstones, and back to our faces. "Art was being funny. I think he was just trying to scare us because it's Halloween."

Fawn shivered and moved into the protected space between the immovable police officer and the patrol car. The officer reached into the back seat, pulled out a blanket, and wrapped it around her shoulders.

Looking at each of us in turn, he asked, "While you were in the cemetery, did you see anyone? Did you hear anything?"

"The wind…," Tucker whispered in a strange, far-off way.

"No," Art broke through Tucker's creepy voice, "I was waving my flashlight around and nothing moved but the trees."

Fawn and I nodded in agreement.

"So how did you find the woman?" Officer Grady asked.

I responded, "It was her shoes. The light from Art's flashlight beamed on her red shoes. Then we saw her legs. At first we thought it was a Halloween prank...that she wasn't real."

Fawn's face tightened and her eyebrows squeezed together. "It was like a horror movie."

"Why don't I call your parents?" Grady opened the car door and took a seat. The four of us circled around the open door like moths circling around the only Coleman lantern in the woods as he relayed our home phone numbers over the police radio.

8

"Okay, hop in. I'll take you home. I want to make sure you get there safely. You'll have to come to the station tomorrow and give us your statements, all right?"

"Yes, sir," Art answered.

For once I was happy to let him speak for all of us.

The next afternoon, Fawn and I had our first chance to be alone together since the grisly events of the night before. I was sprawled sideways across her bed, stomach down, with my head propped up in my hands, my feet dangling over the side. She was watching a video for her book report.

On the cerebral spectrum, we're exact opposites. Fawn has never read a whole book, while I'm a master at speed-reading and consume books voraciously, which explains why I know words like "voraciously", "cerebral", and "spectrum." I make mostly "A's", while a "D" on Fawn's report card draws comments from her parents like, "Not bad."

Fawn sat in an odd position, knees pointing left and right with the soles of her feet touching. She might have been doing a yoga move or she might have been playing footsies with herself.

"We should have gone to Aspinwall," I said, interrupting her concentration. "The houses in town are closer together and there aren't any cemeteries. We could have bagged a lot of candy and missed seeing that dead woman." I shivered. "So how'd we get talked into going trick-or-treating around here, anyway?"

"It was Art's fault."

9

I was thinking the same thing. Day-in and day-out friendship with Fawn since we were five years old had forged our minds into one. Just because Fawn is too shy to say what she thinks and I have a dangerously loose tongue, someone who doesn't know us might assume we have diifferent personalities, but the truth is, we don't.

She was right. It *was* Art Zampini's fault—straight A, know-it-all Art, tormenting me since kindergarten. Now, in the eighth grade, it had come to this: an eyeball-to-eyeball look at a dead woman, spooked-out-of-my-mind, Art-in-my-face kind of Halloween night.

My mind moved on, remembering Fawn lying on the ground. "When you fell face down like that, it's a wonder you didn't break your nose."

"The fake boobs broke my fall," Fawn replied.

I laughed. Both of us had only a hint of boobs. I should say a promise of boobs. We were hopeful that, typical of late bloomers, we would emerge full-bosomed by the age of sixteen. "What did you stuff in that dress anyway?"

"M&Ms wrapped in plastic sandwich bags."

"Oh, call the Wondrous Bra Company! This could be worth a fortune!"

"*What?* I used what I had. My mom was giving out packs of M&Ms to the trick-or-treaters."

"That woman looked so horrible, I almost fainted, too."

"I didn't faint. I tripped on my train."

"Did you see Art's face?"

Fawn nodded.

"It was as white as a ghost!"

"Well, can you blame him? Come on, it isn't everyday you see a dead woman in a tree."

"It wasn't like she just happened to be out walking in the cemetery, accidentally died, and fell in a tree." I paused. "She was *murdered*!"

Fawn shuddered. "I wonder if the person who killed her was lurking in the woods and watched us when we found her. You don't think he was, do you?"

"*He*? What makes you think the murderer was a man?" I asked.

"Women hardly ever murder people. They only think about doing it."

I paused to think about that. *Where does she learn this stuff?*

"Do you think the murderer lives in Dorseyville?" she asked.

"Could that be possible? We know almost everyone who lives here."

"How about Mr. Bartley?"

"Our science teacher? With the glass eye?"

"Well, maybe his good eye is a roving eye."

I laughed, picturing skinny Mr. Bartley chasing after a young blonde in red, high-heeled shoes. "You're nuts, you know that? There isn't a man in Dorseyville young enough or psycho enough to kill that lady. But someone killed her." I paused for a moment,

11

then asked, "I wonder who she is."

"No one from around here, that's for sure."

"Why?"

Fawn gave me her "exasperated with my lack of fashion knowledge" look. "She was big city all over," she explained. "Think about how she was dressed—bangle bracelets, leather mini-skirt, and four-inch heels. If she *had* lived around here, we would have heard of her before this."

"Oh."

Fawn sighed. "Boy, would I love to have a pair of shoes like that."

I nodded in agreement. "They're to die for."

Chapter 3: A High Price to Pay

Five miles away from the countryside of Dorseyville, in the borough of Aspinwall—population 3,233—Eduardo Sanguine drifted away, deep in thought in his art studio.

How they sparkled in the glow of the lamplight that night. The red of them—alizarin crimson—a color so rich and deep, I could scarcely turn my eyes away. At the point where the heels curved away from my view, the reflected light turned from crimson to dragon's blood, a rich, deep red-brown. I could catch that reflection. I knew I could.

The shape of them…the flashing sense of light…a symbol of fire. Four-inch heels elevated the flames that flickered in his mind. He knew when he saw them he would kill to paint those shoes.

13

"Mr. Sanguine," Mrs. Glassport said, catching his attention, "I believe the right side of my face is my best side."

Mr. Sanguine sighed. *What I'd give for a mute model. Her sharp voice drives me to distraction.* "Both sides of your face are equally unsuitable. I will paint you the way *I* see you."

"Well!" Mrs. Glassport sputtered, but she did not move from her set pose. Her ample body overflowed the frail, Rococo-style chair he had placed near the window for her.

"How would you like to eat your paints?" she said.

Her tone sounded hostile. *Not surprising; she's all bulldog.* "Shall we let me be the judge of how to paint this watercolor?" With a sweeping brush stroke of plain water, he slashed her throat across the paper.

His mind wandered. *Now where was I? Oh, yes, the shoes…the sole reason I needed a model, any model, even Mrs. Glassport, a woman of no taste, no redeeming qualities, and an air of haughtiness that drowns my senses like cheap perfume. She is the epitome of what I loathe in people. The fact that I stooped to partner with a woman like her only accentuates the agony of my circumstances.*

"I *do* hope you will capture the exceptional smoothness of my skin. I inherited it from my mother. I don't wear a speck of makeup, you know."

It would take more than a speck of makeup to cover that gaping hole of your mouth. Two, maybe three powder puffs would do it. Reluctantly, he painted over the slash on her neck.

14

Moving his eyes down to the shoes, he sharpened the edges, deepened the shadows, and adjusted a highlight.

She giggled. "What will Adelia Pennycamp say when she hears of this? Wait 'til I tell her I sat for you. That ought to top her claim to fame—being picked to feed Shamu on her trip to Sea World." *Shamu is a step up on the mammal scale from you.* "Squirming only makes you look bigger from here. Do you think you could sit still?"

He painted an allusion of hair, a spritz of background color, added a shadow to one side of her nose, then dry-brushed a few strands of hair. With the handle of his brush, he measured the width of her shoulders. *Immense.*

His eyes returned to the shoes in the painting like a welcome homecoming from a thrashing, tumultuous storm at sea. *Ahhh...they were exquisite.*

"That will do for today," he said, wiping his hands on a paper towel.

"Would you like me to come back tomorrow?"

It would be ideal if you disappeared from the earth tomorrow. "Yes, tomorrow at nine."

"Good day, Mr. Sanguine. It wouldn't hurt you to learn some manners, you know."

"Manners are for idiots," he replied as he waved her out.

Mrs. Glassport returned the next morning, promptly at nine. Mr. Sanguine imagined himself committing unspeakable acts of terror on her until he remembered the shoes...the object of his desire. Reluctantly, he opened the door for her. She entered with far too much noise. Puffing in and out like a heart attack about to happen, Mrs. Glassport walked across the room and dropped into the antique chair. Mr. Sanguine gazed at it sympathetically.

"Whew, it's quite a hike up those stairs," she wheezed. "Six floors and no elevator!"

Let me log that complaint in my mental book of Worthless Women's Habits. "This is my studio, madam, not a home for the handicapped. While it lacks some creature comforts, the light from this large window is essential, and the view from this height allows me to observe living things from a distance, as I prefer."

Using motions to avoid touching her, he attempted to arrange her figure in the same pose it had been in the day before. To shift her derriere to the right, he lowered his cupped hands as if struggling to lift a heavy weight, then he thrust the imaginary weight over and to the right. Mrs. Glassport shifted to the right. To adjust her shoulders, he moved his hands in and out in a motion similar to bread-kneading. A fraction of a second before she shifted too much, he flung his hands up, palms facing her, with his hands flat and rigid. She read this gesture correctly, freezing her bones at his silent command.

At the very moment he felt satisfied that he could proceed with the painting, a dark shadow crossed the floor.

"Get out of my light!" Mr. Sanguine screamed at the window washer. The man outside appeared to hear nothing. Slowly, he continued washing the outside of the glass as if in a trance, wiping his squeegee once across the top, followed by overlapping vertical strokes, and ending with a sweep across the bottom.

Sanguine gestured repeatedly to get his attention, once to go away, once to shake his fist, and once to pull at his own hair. Still, the window washer paid him no attention. Mr. Sanquine paused, looking around his studio and, in a desperate attempt to calm himself, focused on the orderly arrangement of his small world. True, it was only a modest, walk-up studio in the north-facing wing of an apartment building in downtown Aspinwall. It wasn't Paris; it wasn't New York; it wasn't even Pittsburgh.

It's a comedy of fate that I had to be born with talent and worth, only to be confined in a town where a Steelers' game is considered a cultural event.

"Do you like my hair today?" Mrs. Glassport interrupted his thoughts.

Mr. Sanguine never lifted his eyes from the soothing sight of his bed in the corner and the poseable skeleton next to it. "Not nearly as much as the birds would," he replied with a sigh. "I finished painting your head yesterday. I merely have to paint your legs today."

"Oooh, can I look?" she said with a smile, obviously ready to leap off the chair if he gave her so much as a nod.

"You may look along with everyone else when I hang the painting in the gallery!" he snapped. His hand swatted the air to indicate that she was to remain seated. "Could we practice being quiet for the rest of the morning?"

"Well!" she huffed quietly. Under her breath she muttered, "You may be the most noted artist in Aspinwall, but you are no Michelangelo."

"And you, madam, are no Mona Lisa."

The light returned and with it came a fresh look at the painting...and the shoes. Yes, he had painted them exactly the way he remembered them.

Chapter 4: An Unreal Reality

I was up early on Saturday morning hoping to grab a muffin and make a quick getaway. But as luck had it, I wasn't able to slip in and out the kitchen that easily. My mother blocked my way. It was obvious she had been waiting for me. We "had words" and, as usual, it was a no-win situation for me.

"I just said I didn't want eggs for breakfast."

"Don't talk to me in that tone of voice, young lady!" she screamed, clearly in one of her melt-down moods.

I had no desire to escalate the crisis, no desire to see the monster in her.

"I'm sorry," I said, thinking about how I could get out of the house fast.

"*Sorry?* Sorry is what I am for having three kids. I hope some-day you have a daughter just like you!" The venom sprayed out of her mouth with the words. She looked at me with indescribable hatred. *If looks could kill, I'd be dead. Heck, if looks could kill, my mother might be the murderer.*

Things quickly spiraled out of control. When the slap came, I wasn't surprised. Nothing she said or did surprised me anymore. I stood my ground and resisted the urge to rub my stinging cheek.

The phone rang. She picked it up and answered sweetly, "Hello? Oh, hello, Mrs. Anderson. Yes, this is a good time. Oh, no, I'm not busy."

I lowered my eyes and studied my hands—hands that couldn't do anything right in my mother's eyes. I said softly, "I have to go to the library in Aspinwall to work on a paper."

My mother cupped her hand over the mouthpiece and looked at me.

"Can I take the bus with Fawn? Her dad will pick us up. She said I can eat dinner at her house."

She nodded. Her mood had changed, thanks to Mrs. Ander-son. "Be home by nine."

By then, she might be in her "cleaning everything in sight" mood or "busy taking care of the family" mood.

With the exception of my mother, we were a normal family. That is, my father and two older sisters were normal, at least most of the time. Sometimes, my mother even appeared normal. That's what made living in my house so confusing. It was easier for me to escape with a book and read about bizarre people in faraway places and follow the twists and turns in a fantasy story than to make sense of my mother.

I sighed. She belonged in a Harry Potter book. She could have been a magician. Mom was an expert at creating illusions. She possessed a kaleidoscope of facial expressions and could perform a number of amazing tricks. For starters, she could charm neighbors, teachers, and total strangers into liking her. But her best trick by far was her ability to make me disappear.

I opened the back door. Outside, the morning air rushed around me, wrapping me in a cool blanket of relief. I rubbed my cheek, hoping to erase any mark. The last thing I wanted was for Fawn to find out about this. She didn't know about my mother. *Is it possible, then, that she doesn't really know me? No. Fawn knows everything about me...the only me that matters, anyway.*

Chapter 5: A Word to the Wise

"Are they pointing at us?" I asked Fawn, ducking behind a pyramid of melons.

"Yes," she replied, pulling the hood of her electric blue windbreaker forward to hide her face.

I should have known the local women would outnumber the cans of tuna in the Brilliant Market on *this* Saturday morning. The news about the dead woman's body had spread quickly in the six days since Halloween.

"The river is high," said one woman I couldn't see. I knew she was talking about the Allegheny River, which formed the southern boundary of Aspinwall. Watching the river rise and fall was a common pastime.

She added with a tone of concern, "Higher than it should be for this time of the year."

Another replied, "The edge of the water is above the tree line on the islands."

"Trouble comes in threes," another woman said. "First, that dead woman, now the river, what's next?"

"Priscilla Griggs, is that you?" Mrs. Brooks called from the mesh bag brigade of women gathered around the freshly baked bread.

It was no wonder they spotted me. The only market in Aspinwall was narrower than the hallways of Dorseyville Middle School and not long enough for me to throw a ping-pong ball end-to-end. There was no escape.

"Yes, it's me, Mrs. Brooks." I weaseled out of my space and followed the scent of cinnamon buns leading straight to her. Fawn had a close call with the bananas as she followed behind me.

"Aren't you the one who discovered that poor woman's body?"

"I wasn't the only one. Fawn Flodi, Art Zampini, and Tucker Riggoli were with me. We were trick-or-treating."

"See, it's on the front page of the *Herald*," Mrs. Brooks went on, holding the local newspaper up for us to see. "You must have been so frightened."

Fawn peered over my shoulder as we read the headline:

Murdered Woman Found in Tree

"Do they know her name?" I asked Mrs. Brooks.

"Not yet. But it doesn't sound like she was a local woman."

"I told you so," Fawn whispered as she nudged my back.

"What did she look like?" Mrs. Brunelli asked.

"Oh, I don't think these children should talk about it," Mrs. Brooks said quickly. "Unless you want to…."

"No, the police said we aren't allowed to say anything. There's an investigation going on and we will be called as witnesses. And my mother says it could scar us for life if we think too much about it," I answered with a practiced look of innocence.

Mrs. Donnelly nodded. "She's right, you know. I don't want to think about it either."

"But there's a murderer on the loose even as we speak!" Mrs. Brunelli shrilled.

The 20-pound vegetable scale couldn't measure the weight of the tension in the Brilliant Market. The women circled closer and hummed in a nervous exchange of worry and speculation. The newspaper fluttered down, forgotten, landing on the French baguettes in their white paper bags.

Turning, I gave Fawn a push and we silently sauntered up the only aisle in the store. Before leaving, I grabbed a copy of the free *Herald* from the stand.

When the door closed behind us, and we were a good six feet away from the outdoor fruit tables, Fawn sputtered, "*Scarred for life*? Did your mother really say that?"

"No, but it sounded good, don't you think?"

Fawn shook her head, barely hiding her smile. "Priggs, it's a good thing you aren't Catholic."

"Yeah, that's what all the Catholics say." Fawn was a signed, sealed, and delivered Catholic, while I was a part-time Protestant. She quivered at the slightest sin and, for some reason, my actions made her quiver a lot.

We headed for a grassy area under a large oak. The murky, gray sky hung low, the kind of sky that offers a sneak peak of coming attractions. Winter was just around the corner. Fortunately, the wind was calm today. My ear lobes took an intuitive measurement of the air temperature—50 degrees. Not bad. After years of exposure to the four seasons in Western Pennsylvania, consisting of freezing-cold, drizzling-damp, steamy-hot and cool-dry weather, my lobes were as precise as the outdoor thermometers at the Busy Beaver Hardware Store.

Leaning against the wrought iron fence, I pulled out the newspaper and read aloud:

> A dead woman's body was found in the trunk of a hollow tree in Pine Creek Presbyterian Cemetery, Dorseyville. Local middle grade students, who were trick-or-treating in the area, discovered the body on Halloween night. Joe Grubbs, O'Hara Township Police Investigator assigned to this case, said the cause of death appeared to be murder. An autopsy has been ordered and a full investigation is underway. The identity of the woman will be withheld until next of kin can be notified.

"They know her name," Fawn said softly.

"They probably found it in her purse." I continued reading.

Anyone with information about this case is asked to contact the O'Hara Township Police Department.

"Whew-eeee," Fawn whistled. "This is big."

Her face had that "I'm about to drown" look. The fast-moving currents seemed to be pulling at her. Soon, I knew, she would be gasping for air.

"Hey, look at the time. We better get to the library before it closes or we'll never get started on our research. Come on!"

It worked. The dazed look left; Fawn returned. I yanked her coat and took off at a run. She had no choice but to follow me.

We ran for several blocks until we came to one of the three red lights in Aspinwall. Ahead we could see a cluster of buildings that leaned slightly into each other, as if they were whispering secrets. The first in the cluster was Ken's Ice Cream Emporium. Its foundation stone was carved with the date 1929. Ken's had been closed since Labor Day. It was a summers-only business because Ken taught English during the school year. My gaze moved to the next store, the Aspinwall Bookshop. If it were up to me, we would spend the day there, browsing through the new mysteries, but it wasn't up to me; we were on a mission.

The light changed and we crossed the street with the intention of reaching the library at the end of the cluster. Next to the library, however, a window framed in yellow bricks beckoned. The Aspinwall Art Gallery frequently changed the paintings in its windows to capture the attention of people passing by—people more intent on ice cream or books than art. Today, the diversion worked. Fawn and I stopped in our tracks.

"Do you see what I see?" I asked. In the window was a painting of a woman everyone in town knew.

"The shoes," she barely breathed.

"It can't be."

"Isn't that Mrs. Glassport…wearing the red high-heeled shoes?"

"Why would she wear those shoes? She's old enough to be our grandmother."

"It's a sign," Fawn said.

"It's a sign, all right. Let's go in. I want to find out about that painting."

Chapter 6: The Scent of a Murderer

The bells at the top of the carved, wooden door jingled as it opened, causing the woman behind the heavy marble counter to look up. The sound seemed to startle her, but she didn't look half as startled as we did. We entered the gallery together, shoulder-to-shoulder, as one. Fawn's wide eyes said it all.

"Are you girls all right?" she asked.

"No. I mean, yes," I replied. "I mean, we were looking at the painting in the window." A musty smell made up of floor polish and the insides of old trunks gripped my nose.

"Oh," she said, letting out a sigh of relief. "It's a new painting by Eduardo Sanguine. He's famous, you know. That is, he's famous here in *Aspinwall*."

"The woman in the painting looks like Mrs. Glassport."

"I'm not surprised you recognized her. He did a superb job of capturing her profile."

As my eyes adjusted to the dim lighting of the odd-shaped entry room, I began to feel somewhat at ease. Doorways on either side opened into other rooms, revealing white walls with rows of dark paintings, spotlights shining down on each one. It looked as if they had been arranged in a police station line-up. "Do you know anything else about that painting?" I asked.

"It's for sale, but the price may be too steep for you—$5,300."

The woman laid her jewel-framed eyeglasses on the counter.

I choked. "I...I mean we weren't thinking about buying it. We wanted to meet the artist."

"His studio is in the Landmark Apartments on Elm Street."

"Thank you," I said, turning to go.

"But I don't think…."

I turned back at the sound of her voice.

"He doesn't like visitors. Artists are sometimes very strange people. I would stay away from him if I were you."

"But we're interested in his work," I said, batting my eyes for effect.

"Then look at his paintings, but keep your distance from Eduardo Sanguine." Her somber face froze into a tight smile above her folded hands.

The bells above the door jingled, sounding the alarm that Fawn wanted to leave.

Chapter 7: A Clear Path

That evening after dinner, I went to Fawn's house and followed her into her bedroom.

"Okay," she said before I even sat down, "Let's call Art."

I dialed his number and he answered. "Hi, Art. It's us, Priggs and Fawn. We were on our way to the library—"

"You went without us?"

Art sounded annoyed with me, but that was nothing new.

He continued, "We were supposed to be doing our research *together*."

"You interrupted me. We didn't go to the library. We didn't get any further than the art gallery."

"So let me understand this. You and Fawn were going to do the research by yourselves but then you didn't. Why? Because you remembered we are a *project team*?"

30

"Noooooo. Would you listen to me? We saw a painting in the window of the art gallery."

"Oh, you forgot about our research project when you saw *a painting*? What was it—a painting of your favorite rock star?"

"*Art!* Could you shut up for two minutes? It was a painting of the red shoes on the dead woman's feet."

I could hear the sound of air being sucked up.

"*What?*" Art asked in disbelief. "Wait! Let me put you on the speakerphone. I want Tucker to hear this."

I heard a click and, seconds later, the video game noise in the background stopped. I continued, "I know it sounds really weird. It *is* really weird. There's a painting of Mrs. Glassport wearing the red shoes in the gallery. We went in and asked about it. The lady who works there said it was a new painting by an artist named Eduardo Sanguine. And get this—his studio is in Aspinwall."

"It doesn't make sense," Art said.

"What did he say?" she asked, pulling on my arm.

"He said it doesn't make sense," I told her.

"That's what *I* thought," she said.

"No one saw those shoes except us, the police," Art paused, "and one other person—"

Tucker whispered, "The murderer."

Chapter 8: The Game Begins

When I hung up the phone, I relayed to Fawn what Art and Tucker had said, then asked, "What are we gonna do?"

Her face lit up. "Wanna watch the people on the foreign language channel and make up what they're saying?"

"No, I mean about our investigation."

"*We* don't have an investigation. *We* are kids. *We* are not police people," she said with her hands on her hips. Her dark blue denim jeans with the little silver studs around the waist and at the bottom of the slightly flared legs were stunning. Simply stunning.

"Don't you think we should try to find out what happened to that woman?" I asked.

"And how would *we* do that?" She held up her hand. "*Wait!* Whatever you say next is going to drag me in with you, so think before you speak."

"I have no intention of dragging you in," I replied, trying my best to give her an exaggerated look of indignation.

"Oh, come on—"

"Nope, no intention," I insisted.

"Are you telling the truth?"

"Nothing but," I said, raising my right hand in the air.

"Honest?"

"May God make Tucker Riggoli the only man who will marry me if I'm lying."

She sounded relieved. "Oh, good, 'cause my mother will end our friendship if we get into any more trouble."

"That's enough to keep me honest, isn't it?"

She nodded, satisfied.

I paused. "But we could investigate the artist."

Fawn stared at me.

"*What?*" I asked, trying not to look guilty.

She continued to stare at me.

"I didn't want to get married anyway!"

Fawn laughed. "I knew it! Look, be sensible. If he isn't the murderer, then you're playing girl detective for nothing. And if he *is* the murderer, you could get yourself—or *us*—killed. Now would that be worth it? The woman is already dead. There's nothing we can do to help her."

33

I hated to admit it, but she did have a point. "You might be right. Okay, let's say you *are* right."

I knew that I had to drag Fawn in slowly. She was wary of me. *It couldn't be the hundreds of times I'd gotten both of us into trouble, could it?* Like the time I talked her into cutting off her two front pipe-curls right before her sister's wedding…and Fawn was the flower girl! Or the time in the second grade when I convinced her to join me in donating our shoes to orphans during a school charity drive. Our mothers had spent days digging through bags until they found them. With our history, it was no wonder she was skeptical of my plans. I spoke softly, "We don't have to do anything…but what if the murderer strikes again?"

Fawn had that "deer in the headlights" look again. There was a limit to how far I could push her and this was it. Absent-mindedly, she twisted the top off a bottle of "Never on Sunday" sunset-red nail polish. A beauty shop smell filled the room.

"Okay, turn the channel," I said, signaling that I was done badgering her.

She let out a happy chuckle as she picked up the remote.

A man and a woman appeared on the screen in what seemed to be a heated argument in Spanish. The object of the game was to see how long each of us could keep going before one of us laughed. Fawn said it was good practice to prevent us from getting wrinkles when we got older.

She went first, mimicking the voice and mannerisms of the dark-haired male, "Your smell is driving me crazy. Is that 'Evening in

Budapest'?" She raised one eyebrow and then the other at me. I struggled to supress a smile. I paused, then spoke for the frilly-dressed, blonde woman. I flipped my hair back as she did. "No, your nostrils are mistaken. Perhaps it is because of the multitude of handsome hairs I see peaking out of them. I am wearing a new perfume made from the droppings of rare Arctic butterflies." I pursed my lips to look like the woman's but, instead, I may very well have looked like a camel. "But I will forgive you because I adore men who wear pomade."

"*Pomade?* What's pomade?" Fawn rolled on the bed laughing, holding up one hand, trying to protect her wet, red nails.

"It's hair slickener."

She composed her face. "If we keep laughing like this, we're going to have lots of wrinkles in our old age. Honestly, Priggs, where do you come up with those words?"

"It pays to read. You should try it—you might expand your vocabulary. Who knows? You could become a sesquipedalian like me."

"I could not. I was vaccinated for that."

I waited. I knew her curiosity would get the best of her.

"Okay, what's it mean?" she asked.

I was more than happy to enlighten her. "Sesquipedalian: one who uses big words."

"I don't need to read. I can expand my vocabulary just by hanging around you," she said and blew on her nails for effect.

Chapter 9: On the Trail

It was Art's idea to start our investigation today. Fawn had a piano lesson that she seemed a little too happy about, and Tucker was doing chores. So it was only Art and I who rode the bus into town, then raced four blocks to Donner Street. We slowed to a walk as we approached Mrs. Glassport's house, one of many with a turret. The air seemed heavier now. The gingerbread trim, which should have made it look cheerier, did little to disguise it's sinister-looking face.

A sign above the side entrance announced in crisp, Old English letters: "Glassport's Income Tax Services." Although we knew Mr. Glassport was technically the tax man, my mother said Mrs. Glassport checked each tax return "for errors."

36

As we mounted the wooden steps, I looked up at the "G" centered in the stained glass window above the doorway.

"*You* knock," Art said when we reached the door.

"No, *you* knock," I said. "It was *your* idea."

If Art had stuck his tongue out just then, his face would have had that look he usually gives me at times like this. But he didn't. Maybe we had grown beyond the tongue-sticking-out stage. Or maybe he was filled with fear, like I was, for what we were about to do.

Taking a deep breath, he grabbed the brass knocker and rapped twice. The double doors, made of a deep cherry-colored wood, echoed the sound. We waited.

Suddenly, one of the doors flew open.

Mrs. Glassport charged at us verbally. "Don't you kids know that it's suppertime? Do you think you can go around bothering people at all hours? Where are your manners?"

"We're terribly sorry," Art said, bowing his head ever so slightly to show respect.

I could tell he had practiced that move.

"We didn't mean to bother you," he added.

"Well, then, what *do* you want, Art Zampini and Priscilla Griggs, now that my dinner is getting cold?" she asked, but with less force than before.

Purple spandex stretched before me as she walked over and bent down to pick up the Pittsburgh Post Gazette on the porch. *So much give in those pants...it really is amazing*, I thought.

"We saw the painting of you in the art gallery," he said.

"You did? Did you like it?"

"We did," he replied.

"Well, come in." She stood aside and held the door open for us. "We can't stand out in the cold discussing fine art now, can we?" she asked, her dinner apparently forgotten.

We entered a foyer, turned left, and followed her into a room that in Victorian times had probably been a parlor. High ceilings curved down at the corners to meet rough plastered walls.

"How did you become the model for the painting?" Art asked, sinking deeply into the green velvet cushions of her Queen Anne sofa.

Mrs. Glassport seemed enthralled with his every word, which gave me a chance to look around. At the edges of a flower- and leaf-patterned rug, I could see a blackened wood floor. It was an old house, sure to have three floors and a basement. I didn't need to tour her house to know that; it was a typical Aspinwall mansion tucked in a town full of century-old mansions, all waiting for the remake of a Frankenstein movie.

"I was asked to sit for the painting by Mr. Sanguine himself," I heard her practically mew to Art. "I don't know why he wanted me, of all people, but the results show that he knows what he's doing."

The furniture appeared heavy, immovable. A dark, built-in bookcase contained volumes of what I call "lookers"—books that some people look at but no one reads. A set of sea creatures and mermaids made out of glass rested on the top shelf. Over the heavy, brick fireplace was a wooden plaque, carved with the words 'Home, Sweet Home.' *She probably uses that for a dart board.* Glowing in the corner was a lamp on a tall post, with light squeezing out of the openings in the intricate design of its frosted globe.

"It's a very good likeness of you," Art said, laying on the charm that he usually saves for our teachers. "Do you know the artist?"

"Do I *know* him? Well, I spent enough hours in his studio. Not that it was easy to get to! Six floors up. And with my high blood pressure—"

Art jumped in quickly to keep Mrs. Glassport from drifting away from our topic of interest. "What's he like?"

"Obnoxious! Eduardo Sanguine couldn't fill a thimble with his personality. He is crude and rude, without any manners whatsoever." She paused to catch her breath. "But as a painter, he's huge. Did you notice the graceful way he painted my hands? As delicately as a Renoir, I think."

"Yes, it *is* something," Art said.

I lowered my head to hide my face at that, knowing if I caught Art's eye, we would break into laughter.

"I noticed the shoes in the painting," I said, trying to look serious. "Are they yours?"

"Heavens, no. I haven't worn shoes like that in more than...several years. In fact, I didn't see those shoes in the studio when I was sitting for him. Mr. Sanguine must have added them later. I don't know why he painted me wearing them...unless he envisioned the younger woman in me. An artist can do that, you know."

"I'm sure he could," he answered with a nod. "Thank you for talking with us. I'm sorry about interrupting your dinner." He stood up to go.

"Don't mention it. It was delightful to talk to a couple of young art fans. Tell your mother I said she should take you to the Frick Fine Art Gallery in Carnegie one of these days. They have a marvelous collection I think you would enjoy."

"We will, Mrs. Glassport. Thanks again."

I followed him out and down the stairs. "Goodbye and thank you," I called over my shoulder. I breathed in the cold, fresh evening air.

When we reached the streetlight, I couldn't stand the suspense any longer. "So what did we learn?" I asked.

"She doesn't like Eduardo Sanguine," he replied.

"No, duh. She doesn't like a lot of people."

He stopped, looked thoughtful, and said, "We learned something else."

"What's that?" I asked.

"She's not the murderer."

He walked on without explaining, leaving me to stare at the back of his Steelers' parka.

Chapter 10: Library Plot

"Look! It says she was an actress," I said with the excitement we all felt at finding the *Herald* in the school library on Monday morning. We had been waiting anxiously all week to see if there would be another article about the murder.

Art began to read it out loud:

No More Encores for Leading Lady

The murder victim, found by local students on October 31st in Pine Creek Presbyterian Cemetery in Dorseyville, was identified as Atalia Trinski, 28. An acclaimed actress, Ms. Trinski was in Pittsburgh to play the role of the leading lady in the production of *Les Miserables* at the Benedom Center Theatre. Born Marlene Gludsky in Boston, Massachusetts, she

41

took the stage name of Atalia Trinski early on in her career.

"Atalia Trinski," Fawn mouthed the words, as if trying on her name.

"Shhhh!" Mrs. Storkle, the head librarian scowled at us, giving the 'shhhhh' extra emphasis by raising her shoulders. "Do you kids want to go back to study hall?"

We shook our heads and assumed the lock-down position—quiet students just doing our homework. Only Tucker was seriously working as he searched for Captain Bridgeway in the encyclopedia, all the while biting his lower lip.

Mrs. Storkle moved away from us. Her feathery-white hair swished from side-to-side with each step. Zigzagging through the stacks, she returned to the circulation desk, where she dropped a misplaced book. The diamond pendant dangling from the gold chain around her neck proved that only the best would do for Mrs. Storkle. She would never stoop to our level. She expected us to rise to hers.

With lowered eyes, we watched her bird-like legs head toward us again, turn suddenly, and disappear into her office. We shifted our chairs and leaned forward in a tight huddle.

"Why did her shoes show up in that painting?" I asked softly.

Fawn bubbled up, "It's obvious those shoes did not belong to Mrs. Glassport."

I noticed, not for the first time, that Fawn had a gift for stating the obvious.

In a whisper, Art continued:

> She was found wearing a white sweater, black
> leather skirt, and red high-heeled shoes. The motive
> for the murder does not appear to be burglary, as
> Ms. Trinski's purse was found nearby with money
> and credit cards intact.

"She's not from around here, just like we thought," Fawn bubbled up. "If she was, she'd know better than to go out at night without a coat."

"It *is* odd that she wasn't wearing a coat," Art agreed. After a pause, he said, "The artist who painted that picture must have seen this woman in her red shoes. Could he have murdered her?"

"The shoes in the painting aren't proof," Tucker whispered.

Art nodded. "You're right. There could be lots of red shoes that look like that. It could be just a coincidence."

"Is it a *coincidence* that the shoes in the painting are an exact match to the shoes we all saw," I asked, "right down to the swirling design on the heels, and that someone as old as Mrs. Glassport is modeling them?" I didn't wait for an answer. "*Not!*"

Fawn added: "Nobody's safe if the murderer lives here."

"Maybe we should check out the artist," I said, thinking that Art had the most gorgeous brown eyes.

His eyebrows went up. "You girls should stay away from him."

That ruined the moment. "Oh, so now I'm a girl. Why don't you make up your mind? When it comes to talking to Mrs. Glassport or washing my face in the snow, I'm just another guy."

"That was in the first grade!" Art said, outraged.

"Did you think I would forget?"

"I always did have to knock a little sense into that hard head of yours," he said, showing his dimple with a smile that melted me.

I ignored the insult and his smile. "But when it comes to smoking out the murderer, now I'm a girl."

"Smoking out the murderer…" Fawn repeated with her eyes wide. "Wow, you sound like a TV cop."

"If you think you can do it without me, Pini, go ahead." I threw down a challenge. "How about girls against guys?"

"Priggs, this isn't the time to go off on your own," Art replied. "Anything we do, we should do together. All of us found the body together, didn't we?"

Fawn and Tucker nodded and, finally, I did, too.

"Okay, so we stick together," Art said. "Now I have a plan…."

We leaned our heads closer together and listened.

Chapter 10: In the Artist's Lair

The early morning light in the studio was crisp and bright as Eduardo Sanguine put the finishing touches on Trudy Talbot's hair.

"My arm is aching." Trudy said.

Funny, he thought, *how does one's arm ache when it's missing?* Propped with her right shoulder against the back of the chair, the amputated stump was not visible from his viewpoint. It was just the way he wanted it.

Arms were insignificant to him, both the one held closely to her side and the one on the other side that wasn't in the left sleeve of her drab green, unlined jacket. When he first saw this uni-armed woman outside the J & W Variety Store, he knew he had reached a new low in desperation. She was as colorless as squid, with deep-set eyes, and an asymmetrical, slightly angular jaw. On impulse, he had asked her to sit for him. Later that night, he had questioned his sanity but, in the end, it was working out.

He focused his mind on his work. The first of two lion head clasps on the beaded purse in the painting required his total attention. "Concentric abstract shapes depict the reflection of light in the polished gold. There, like that. Perfect!" He remembered the way the purse had looked. He had never seen such an exquisite pair of lion heads, one male and one female. With a final stroke, he said more to himself than to her, "That will do for today."

Miss Talbot stood up, walked to the door, hesitated, then turned back to face him. "Mr. Sanguine? Did you say you would pay me after each sitting or not until all of the sittings are completed?" She clutched her badly worn, black vinyl bag in her right hand as if her life depended on it.

"*Money?* You want to talk about *money?* Can you *not* see that I am in the midst of painting a masterpiece?" His voice seemed to gather strength as her body shrank away from him. "We will discuss payment for your services when my mind is free to think of such things. Now get out of here. And don't come back until tomorrow morning at nine."

She disappeared from the room before he finished speaking as if the strong wind of his words had carried her off.

Chapter 11: The Gallery Whispers

On Saturday morning, I arrived at Fawn's house at ten in the morning. I walked around the side of the house and knocked on the metal doorframe.

Mrs. Flodi yelled from the kitchen, "Come on in, Priggs."

I pulled the storm door open and turned the handle to the back door. Sammy, Fawn's hyperactive black poodle, met me with licks and yelps.

"Hi, Sammy," I said, kneeling down to rub his curly mop. I loved Sammy as if he were my own dog. Not that he could be mine. My mother viewed dogs as the opposition to a clean and tidy house. *You can get too carried away with clean, I say.* but I'd never dare to say it to my mother.

47

"Would you like a piece of cherry cobbler? I just made it."
Mrs. Flodi smiled broadly. Then she remembered her shyness and
pursed her lips to cover an overbite of teeth. She giggled.

I almost inhaled the sour cherries with the crunchy, cinnamon
crust through my nostrils. Fawn's mom baked fabulous desserts
that she never ate. Weighing slightly more than 100 pounds, she
stood only a little higher than my shoulder. Her life was spent doting on Fawn, her second child born to her rather late in life. Fawn's
sister had married years earlier and moved away. It seemed to me
that Mrs. Flodi wished for more children, because she had practically adopted me.

Fawn's mom was Italian; her dad, Hungarian. Her parents were
passionate people who argued about Italian versus Hungarian food,
music, gardening, styles of furniture, and cars. By comparison, my
parents, of German and Scottish descent, were practical and boring people who logically discussed the price of gas or meat and the
durability of just about everything else.

"No, thank you. I just had breakfast. Is Fawn here?"

"In her bedroom. Go on back."

The one-story house was small and cozy. A hallway led to the
bedrooms. As I approached Fawn's room, I could see her through
the open door. I stopped a few feet away. The show in progress
seemed too good to miss. I didn't want Fawn to know she was
being watched.

Fawn belted out the lyrics to a CD, swept one arm up under
her long, brown mane of hair and tossed it into the air. She danced

happily, with passion. Her cheeks glowed, giving a pink tinge to her tan, slightly olive skin, and her eyes sparkled. Watching in the wings, I admired her razzle-dazzle. I envied her simple way of looking at life, her true belief in herself and other people, her dog, and her doting mom.

She wiggled a well-practiced, snappy two-step. One hip swung to the left with such force that it banged without mercy against the dresser, rattling a very girlish pink and white lamp.

"Owww!" Fawn cried out, rubbing her jeans on the left side.

Laughter rolled out of me.

Fawn laughed, too, still rubbing her hip.

"You should have seen yourself! Hollywood, get ready for your next star!"

"I'll get you for this. Why didn't you tell me you were there?" she asked.

"What? And miss the show of a lifetime? I didn't know you could sing like that."

"I'm more than just a pretty face, you know," she said.

"Yes, you are! If you can't out-sing the competition, perhaps you can bump them off the stage."

"Go get her, Sammy." Fawn laughed as the little poodle jumped on the bed. She plopped down beside the dog and nuzzled her face into his fur.

I settled into the pillows on the opposite side. "Wanna go to the library?" I asked. "My dad's driving into town this afternoon."

"It's raining; what the heck? There's nothing better to do.

Maybe I can go to the drug store and buy this new mascara that
Teen Scene magazine says will make our eyelashes grow an inch."

"Do you really believe that?" I asked, but I knew she did.
"First, we'll go and do our research on Captain Bridgeway. Then
the drugstore, okay?"

She rolled her eyes and smiled. "Dead men don't interest me.
But lead the way!"

A crowd huddled close together under a colorful assortment
of open umbrellas in front of the Art Gallery. We couldn't help but
notice them as we approached the library. Grabbing Fawn's arm,
I steered us through an opening to see what the attraction was.

A new painting was on display in the window. The subject
seemed to arouse anger in the crowd. I gasped.

"How rude!" exclaimed Mrs. Baumgartner.

"Is that the artist's idea of a joke?" Mrs. Hall asked. "To use a
poor, disabled woman like Miss Talbot in that manner...putting
lions in a painting of a woman with a missing arm."

A woman I didn't know spoke up: "The lions make a mock-
ery of her tragic misfortune."

Another added, "Who would paint her that way? Look at the
sign below the painting. It says the artist is Eduardo Sanguine. *The
Lions Roar*, that's the title."

Painted in sharp focus, two lions' heads, one with a full mane,
and one without, formed the clasps on the the expensive-looking
handbag covered in beads. The purse was exquisiste in rays of

sunlight, in contrast to the woman in the shadows, who was less prominent but painted with enough distinction so that there could be no question about the model's identity. It was clearly Miss Talbot, a woman known to all us as the one-armed cashier in the J&W Variety Store.

Mrs. Baumgartner shuddered. "I remember the accident like it was yesterday. Remember, Lois, when we were kids?"

"Yes, I do. The circus had just opened down at the baseball field. When she reached in to pet that lion, he grabbed her arm and wouldn't let go. I heard a piercing scream. When I turned to look, she was shaking all over, her clothes soaked in blood. We wondered if she was going to live, poor dear. Those lion heads *do* bring back the memories."

"Why would that artist paint her that way?" asked Mr. Zoran.

I pulled Fawn back from the crowd so abruptly, her umbrella dipped to the ground, leaving her standing in the rain with her hair beginning to wave. "A woman who lost her arm like that would never wear a purse with a lion on it."

"Besides, how could she afford to buy an expensive designer handbag like that?" she asked.

"Fawn," I said, clutching her coat, "does this seem similar to the painting of Mrs. Glassport and the red shoes? Here's a woman we know wearing something that obviously doesn't belong to her. Think about it. Who owned the red shoes? Who owns the purse?"

Her eyes got that flashbulb look. "Call Art!"

I dialed his number from Fawn's cell phone.

51

"Arthur Zampini speaking."

"Art?"

"Is this the girl who can't get enough of me?" he asked.

"No such girl exists! It's me, Priggs. There's a new painting you gotta see in the Art Gallery—by Eduardo Sanguine. Fawn and I just saw it on our way to the library."

"Why didn't you call me and Tucker so we could go with you?" Art asked.

I cut him off before he had a chance to annoy me. "Yeah, yeah, well, I'm calling you now. Can you two get down here and take a look at it?"

"We can hitch a ride with my mom. She's going to the market."

"It's in the window. You'll know what I mean as soon as you see it. I think another woman's been murdered."

Chapter 13: A Step Too Far

The following Saturday, I sat on the bench at the bus stop on Elm Street. I was waiting for my dad to have his tires rotated at Ed's Auto Repair next door. At the last minute, I had asked if I could go into town with him. *Anything's better than being held captive on a Saturday with Mom.*

My gaze traveled across the street, attracted by the motions of a man with a squeegee, poised on an extension ladder, cleaning a sign that said "Landmark Apartments."

Maybe it was Art's endless jabs. Maybe it was defiance. Maybe it was simple curiosity. Later, it might be easy to say "should have, would have, could have" but, at that moment, the very moment when I could have changed my destiny, I got up and started walking. I ran across the street. The time for thinking had come and gone so quickly, I missed it.

The yellow brick building on the corner rose up six stories. It was much younger than the other structures around town, one of the newer 1950s buildings. I pushed hard on the glass door and boldly walked into a small entryway. Through a large glass window ahead of me, I could see a square garden, with the building wrapping around it on all sides. Along the wall to my right was a row of mailboxes. I scanned the names until I found the one I was looking for: E. Sanguine, #602.

Pressing only the tips of my toes down on the brown, speckled tiles, I moved with grace of a ballerina into the hallway. Looking up, I scanned the winding pattern of stairs. *No bodies...I mean, no people. Good! If Eduardo Sanguine should see me, I'll look like an innocent kid. At least I can tell Art and Fawn and Tucker I found out where his studio is. What can happen?*

My pep talk did the trick. I placed one foot on the first step, slowly pressing my weight on it to check for sound. The steel grids gave no complaint. If I was careful not to let my shoes clack, I could ascend like a ghost. I proceeded slowly.

Four-and-a-half flights up, I felt out of breath. My heart pounded in a triple beat that shouted in my ears: "go-no-more, go-no-more."

I turned the corner and stepped up to the fifth floor landing just as the door marked "Exit" flew open. A bushy-haired man in a black trench coat rushed forward. As his coat brushed against my legs, I hurriedly stepped backwards to get out of his way. My foot tripped on the steel grating of the step, setting off a loud clang, as my weight shifted backwards. I could feel myself falling. Blindly, I grabbed at the air. My left wrist hit the banister. My hand flailed, finally making contact. I wrapped my fingers securely around the cold steel railing. Noise reverberated throughout the entire column of twelve sets of stairs.

"I'm so sorry," he said in a voice so deep and full that it echoed "sorry, sorry, sorry" from every direction. He reached out to grab me.

Hastily, I stood up and waved my hand to indicate that it was nothing; I was okay.

Please, God, don't let him be Eduardo Sanguine. Don't let him follow me. The man paused for a second, gave me a puzzled look and said no more.

I turned to step up. He hurriedly descended the stairs in the opposite direction.

Okay, breathe. In, out, in, out. Pound, pound, pound, pause, pound. I climbed more steps.

On the landing at five-and-a-half floors, I stopped and puffed out what felt like the clatter of rattling chains in my chest. Whew! That had scared the sweetness out of me. What would I do if I encountered Mr. Sanguine? Maybe I should go back.

Out of nowhere, the voices of Art and the woman in the gallery taunted me: "*This isn't the time to go off on your own...you girls should stay away from him.*"

I shook my head, inhaled deeply and placed my foot firmly on the next step, lifting my weight with a slight swing to my hip. When I reached the final landing, I opened the door in slow motion and peered into a dark hallway.

602, 602, 602.

The carpet on the floor now softened my footsteps. I passed a door with the number 600 on it. The next door down was partially open. *Hmmm, what to do, what to do?* The part of me that might have run was overtaken by the part of me that did not know the meaning of the word run. Instead, I looked up and down the hallway, which turned and continued at either end. *Are there more apartments around those corners?* With moves copied from TV detectives, I approached 602 with stealth and cunning. Hugging the wall, I stopped outside the open door.

I heard voices inside and, hardly breathing, I listened. I recognized the woman's voice. *Mrs. Storkle? The school librarian? What's she doing here?*

Chapter 14: Artist Meets Perfectionist

I overheard Mrs. Storkle saying, "Mr. Sanguine, I must say I am surprised at your studio—stacks of paper, open books with their spines bent and broken, and that mess of art supplies scattered haphazardly on the counter. How can you work in such a disorganized place?"

"I don't work in a place, madam. I work in my mind which, I can assure you, is exceptionally well-organized," Mr. Sanguine replied in a civil tone.

As he returned to his painting, he seemed to be talking to himself, "The brilliance of light sparkled...fractured into a hundred lights over those earrings. If I paint the colors in a circular rainbow, I can capture their glowing hues."

Suddenly, Sanquine barked, "Did I tell you to move? How do you expect me to paint a moving target?"

Through the crack in the door, I could see her eyes widen, but she said nothing.

"That face...what a challenge," the artist said under his breath. He moved around the room as if studying it from different positions.

Possibly, Mrs. Storkle mistook his words for a compliment because the corners of her thin-lipped mouth curled up ever so slightly. "It's awfully warm in here," she whined.

I had to give it to her; she was gutsy. After his last outburst, I wouldn't have said another word.

Sanguine walked over to the window, unlocked it, and heaved it open. As he turned back, the wind blew the door open further, causing him to look in my direction. For a split second, I thought he saw me. I leaned back against the wall and froze. I heard him take long strides to where his paints lay. He stopped. I heard him pick up his brush. I relaxed. *No, he hadn't seen me.*

"Mrs. Storkle, keep your eyes on the far wall. Lift your chin— to the left. That's it. Now hold it. *Do* not *move*." I watched him pick up a mirror, which he used to examine Mrs. Storkle's face. He shifted his body position and his back blocked my view of her.

Heavy footsteps approached from the hallway around the corner, accompanied by a banging/clanging sound. I made a dash for stairwell, exiting through the door. I hid behind it as it closed, listening, shaking.

The rhythm of the footsteps continued. Closer, closer they came. I held my breath. They passed by the stairwell door and continued down the hall away from me. I cracked the door open ever so slightly and caught a glimpse of the back of a man in a white jumpsuit, a utility bucket banging against his leg as he walked on. Suddenly, Mr. Sanguine stepped into the hallway, his gaze focused on something lying on the gray carpet. He walked over to it, reached down, and picked up a small magazine with a splashy red and yellow cover showing an overly made-up woman. "*Playhouse Digest,*" he mumbled. "Who dropped this?"

The mirror fell from his hand to the floor and smashed, scattering bits of light in all directions. "Indeed!" he bellowed aloud to the empty hallway. "She's a model to kill for."

Chapter 15: Dead On

A model to kill for? I tiptoed down one flight of stairs, then ran toward the garage as fast as my mind could race. *Did I hear him right? Who did he mean? Mrs. Storkle? Why would he want to kill her? Was he the murderer? Was she in danger? Should I call the police? Should I tell my dad? He might be mad at me if he knew I went up there without telling him.*

"The car is ready, Sweetie," my dad said, putting his wallet into his pocket. "Where'd you go?"

"Oh, I thought I saw someone I knew. I went over to say 'Hi,' but it wasn't her." Amazing, how I could roll out made-up answers even under stress.

As we drove away, I saw Mrs. Storkle coming out of the front door of the Landmark Apartments. I sighed with relief.

The following day after school, I convinced Fawn to get off the bus with me at the Pine Creek Presbyterian Cemetery.

"I can't believe I let you talk me into coming back here," she said, timing her footsteps to leap over each marker she encountered. Sunk two inches below the ground, the flat slabs waited like traps for unsuspecting tourists.

"We had to come back," I replied. "We have to get a rubbing of Captain Bridgeway's headstone, remember?"

"Why couldn't "we" be Art and Tucker?"

"Because."

Fawn stopped and looked at me. "You don't have an answer. That's a first!"

"Okay, I admit it. I wanted to take another look at the place to see if the murderer left any clues."

"If you had told me that, I'd still be home, curled up, watching cartoons."

"I know you so well," I said, smiling. "Look, this cemetery doesn't seem so bad in the daylight."

"That tree still looks like something out of a horror movie."

"Yes, it does, doesn't it? Come on," I took off at a run, leaping like a gazelle over flat slabs and smaller headstones.

She followed closely, as I knew she would.

Near the Death Tree, we slowed to a walk. It looked as if a giant hand had snapped the top off, leaving sharp, jagged points sticking up twelve feet into the air. The crusty trunk appeared to a solid mass but, as we walked around it stepping carefully over its charcoal black roots, the tree revealed a gaping hole. Its guts were missing, as if scooped out by some mysterious force. Termites had carved out the seat of a throne, leaving spots of fresh, caramel-colored sawdust.

Fawn shuddered. "Wow, that's creepy. Why don't *you* look for clues, while *I* look for the headstone?"

"Okay. There's a big piece of brown paper in my backpack. And the chalk is in the pocket," I replied.

Finding what she needed, she walked away.

I leaned into the opening of the trunk, feeling like I was putting my head into a guillotine. *Whack!* That's the sound I expected to hear any minute.

"Whoa!" Fawn yelled, as she lost her balance on a large slab. "These suckers are slippery!"

"It's disrespectful to walk on them," I yelled back.

"No kidding! James Kozur II just tried to grab me."

Twigs, old leaves, sawdust, sticky stuff, and a rotten wood smell inhabited the tree, but no clues. I backed my nose out.

"Bridgeway—here it is, " she called out. "Alexander or Andrew?"

"Andrew!" I shouted, making my way around the tree as I brushed my hiking boots lightly over the grass, looking for any clues that might be hidden there. After completing my search, I yelled, "There's nothing here."

I shaded my eyes with my hand. Scanning the cemetery in all directions, I looked for any signs of movement. In the distance, the bare trees and pines came alive, swaying first this way, then that, as if doing the wave. The wind carried with it a crisp, wintery smell and, like a rush of pure oxygen, it heightened my senses. All the blue had faded from the sky, leaving only a Confederate gray. I had the eery feeling that human eyes were peering back at me through the deep, dense underbrush. Suddenly, a black cat leaped out of the forest. I jumped. He crept away along the tree line. *Stalking, that's what he's doing. Better not mention it to Fawn. She sees omens in ordinary things.*

"Here it is!" she yelled.

Relieved at the sound of her voice, I ran to the headstone where Fawn.was struggling to rub the name onto the paper. The edges were flapping rapidly against the slate, tapping out a drum roll. "Want me to hold the paper for you?"

"That would be nice."

I kept one eye on the woods as she rubbed over the letters: CAPTAIN ANDREW BRIDGEWAY. The wind tickled my nose. Turning my head so I wouldn't sneeze on her, I noticed the headstone next to it also had the name "Bridgeway." The first name was Alexander. Below the name were carved the words: Private First Class, 1843-1915. "I wonder if these two are related."

"Maybe they're brothers," she offered.

"Could be. Let's take a rubbing of that headstone, too."

"Sure, but why do more work than we have to?"

"I don't know...I'm just curious." I held the brown paper as she rubbed a piece of blue chalk over the carved letters.

"Done. Now let's get out of here."

"We didn't find anything," I murmured.

Fawn took off running toward the street. "Sometimes *not* finding anything is a good thing!"

The next morning, I realized how right she was. The four of us had agreed to meet in the school library for first period study hall, but I was running late and for the worst of reasons; my hair did twirlies on the sides. Not waves, not wisps, but twirlies. Earlier, while getting ready for school, I thought I could transform my straight, shoulder-length blonde icicles into the tropical, breeze-blowing curls worn by the bikini-clad model on the cover of *Hairstylin'* magazine. But it wasn't possible.

That's all I was thinking about when I walked into the school library. I wasn't thinking about what day it was or why we had planned to meet on this particular morning until I saw the shocked faces of Fawn, Art, and Tucker staring up at me. I walked over to the table and picked up the *Herald*.

The headline screamed:

Second Actress Found Dead

Duck bumps fluttered up my arms like fingers running over a piano keyboard, traveled over my shoulders, and raced down my spine. I gulped down a sick feeling in my throat.

"Is this…is she…?" I asked.

Fawn, Art and Tucker nodded in unison.

"Maybe it isn't…," I offered, lamely.

Art raised one eyebrow.

"Ummm," I said, unable to think.

"It says they found a purse, but it doesn't mention any clasp," Fawn explained.

"My dad," whispered Tucker.

"What about your dad?" Art asked.

"He works in the O'Hara Township Police Station. In accounting," Tucker said softly.

"Could we ask him about the purse?" Fawn asked.

Tucker shrugged.

Art knew, as we all did, that the situation had become urgent. "We've got to stop that artist before he paints another portrait."

In the suspense of the moment, I decided not to mention my visit on Sunday to Mr. Sanguine's studio. I would save that for later. No point in getting my already-spooked team of detectives riled up on a bad hair day.

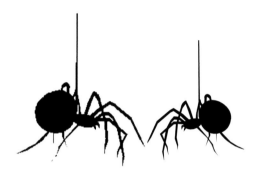

Chapter 16: A Lesson in Fear

The next day, ten minutes before the start of our fourth period art class, Art sat down in the seat next to mine.

"After school," he said, "we'll tell our parents we're going to the Aspinwall Library to do research. We'll get off the bus at the Landmark Apartments and go up to the artist's studio. We'll tell Sanguine we're reporters for the school newspaper and we want to do a story on him. Got it, Priggs?"

"Yeah, yeah, yeah," I answered. *Why does he repeat everything to me like I'm stupid or something?* I hardly looked up from my notebook, where I was concentrating on doodling my name in five different colors.

"Priggs, are you listening to me?"

"Do I look like I'm listening to you?"

"No, you look like a silly girl."

I sighed. Sometimes I think we are like two spiders that continuously weave a spell over each other—a spell that's not entirely comfortable—but one that will bind us together forever. I drew two spiders in black over my red name. We might have gone on arguing that way if we hadn't been interrupted by the voice of our school principal, Mrs. Kappa.

"Class, may I have your attention, please?" she asked. "I'd like to introduce our guest artist."

I looked up and almost fell out of my seat.

"We are delighted to have Mr. Sanguine with us today. He is famous throughout this area."

Mr. Sanguine? What's he doing here? Is he looking for me? No, it couldn't be! I'm positive he didn't see me in the hall outside his studio.

He gave a half-hearted bow.

Mrs. Kappa smiled at him appreciatively. "I will leave you all now in his capable hands. I know you will enjoy his art instruction." She turned and walked out of the room. The steel door shut with a bang behind her.

"If I had a choice, I wouldn't be here!" he bellowed.

I lowered my eyes at the sound of his booming voice.

"But I *don't* have a choice. I am required to teach art to eighth graders in return for the privilege of using the Aspinwall Gallery for my one-man show." He walked to the blackboard and with a piece of gray pastel chalk, wrote his name in large letters: Mr. E. Sanguine.

He turned toward us, leaned forward, and continued. "I don't expect you to learn anything. I don't expect you to know anything. I only expect you to sit in your seats—got that? No one moves until the bell rings!"

He turned and faced his easel. "Oh, spare me," he muttered, shaking his head.

Art's eyes opened wide as he gave me a sharp elbow nudge. I nodded in a superior way, for once knowing something that he didn't. We both knew better than to say anything.

In spite of my nervousness, yes, even fear, I found myself caught up in the pleasure of watching Mr. Sanguine work. A languid body emerged, languid as in Roman bath times, reclining on a sofa of flowing blue silk. Her skin became luminous from the light beaming in from the arched window behind her, its shutters thrown open wide.

He explained how the lines from the arched window merged with the lines of the shutters to draw the viewer's eye to the woman. I followed the lines until I was completely mesmerized. It was as if he had taken me out of this mundane classroom to a place so magical that I believed I *was* the woman in the painting. I stretched my legs out under my desk in what I thought was a languid imitation of hers. Who could not be caught up in his visionary talents?

Jane Boarts, that's who.

68

"Mr. Sanguinie," she called, raising her hand with a spasmodic shake. "Would it be okay if I went to the girls' room?"

His voice bellowed loud enough to shake the easel. "Sanguin-ie? My name is not Sanguin-ie! It is Eduardo Sanguine. *Mr.* Sanguine. *Count* Sanguine, even. But never, *never, do you hear me,* is it pronounced '*Sanguin-ie*', like the blue plate special at the likes of the Little It-*ly* Restaurant in Sharpsburg!!!"

Oh, she shuddered all right. No more thoughts of the bathroom for her, or for any of us, for that matter.

I could see his rage. I could feel the intensity of his emotions. I could almost taste the hatred with which he spat upon all people. And on some level, I understood it. I had experienced that rage from my mother, had felt it in myself.

Mercifully, the bell rang. Jane was the first to escape, followed by everyone in the class.

As I gathered up my books, Art winked at me like a conspirator and whispered he would see me after school.

I wanted to take a closer look at the finished sketch on the easel. I was drawn to it, as a vulture is drawn to a carcass. If I were a vulture, however, what did that make Mr. Sanguine? I took comfort in the thought that he didn't know who I was, had not seen me the day I came to spy on him. I walked slowly to the front of the room.

"Ahhh, one not so easily frightened," he said to me.

"It's beautiful," I said in a breathy whisper, more to the easel than to him.

"That it is," he replied. "Do you like art?"

"Yes, I love it," I admitted. "Not that I have great talent, like you."

"Talent is nothing. Devotion...*that* is everything."

I raised my eyes to his, surprised at his soft words. Did he have a human side, after all? His head had a massiveness to it, with an abundance of dark, almost black, wavy hair encircling it. The same wavy curls repeated in bushy eyebrows above his midnight black eyes.

"What is your name?" he asked.

I didn't see anything menacing about him. I had to remind myself that I could be facing a murderer. "Priggs—Priscilla Griggs, I mean."

"Do you like school?"

"I hate the slow pace of school. I don't like being treated like a child. I don't like bells and schedules. And I don't like kids who can't read." I stopped, drew in a breath, and covered my mouth with my hand. *Where had that come from?* I had never spoken to an adult in such a manner.

To my amazement, he threw back his head and laughed—a deep, rolling laugh. "We have much in common. May I see your artwork?"

I blushed, embarrassed to show him my meager drawings. I opened my binder and explained what I had tried to achieve, even though the results were disappointing. I pointed out my mistakes, but I was sure he had noticed them on his own.

He listened intently, with a depth of understanding I had never felt with a teacher before. His hands touched the paper with his long, finely formed fingers in a way that can only be called tenderness.

He studied my work. "Drums. Nothing but drums. Where are the piccolos?"

"Piccolos?" I repeated, not having any idea what he was talking about.

"Piccolos—small flutes. Imagine that you, the artist, are painting a symphony. The drums are the dark, heavy shapes that give it depth, weight, and a serious tone. You have plenty of drums, but you need the high-pitched, tinkling notes to give your work sensitivity and joy. If you're going to paint a symphony, don't forget the the highlights—the piccolos."

Wow. How easily I was caught up in his magical web.

"Would you like to come to my studio for private art lessons?"

"No, I couldn't," I said quickly, coming back to earth. "You see my parents don't have the money—"

"For free, an exchange. I will teach you if you will let me paint you." He left the offer there, waiting.

He studied my face carefully and seemed to count every second that I delayed. It was as if he knew I would accept. That is, I suppose, how the vulture-eater waits.

I thought about Pini. *Taking lessons could be a better plan because I'd be in the artist's studio.* "Yes, Mr. Sanguine, I will. Thank you."

"Saturday then? Here's my card. It has the address of my studio in Aspinwall. An hour of lessons, an hour of sitting. How about nine in the morning—can you make it?"

I nodded.

"I'll be waiting for you."

Chapter 17: Facing the Facts

After school, Art was impatiently waiting for me on the covered walkway just outside the school entrance. I told him about being invited to Mr. Sanguine's studio and the deal we had struck.

"You can't go there alone!" he ordered.

"Why not?" I countered, putting one hand on my hip.

"*Why not?*" Pulling a copy of the *Herald* from his backpack, he said, "Marie Anna Gephardt, that's *why not!*"

I grabbed the paper from his hand. "*...understudy and replacement for Atalia Trinski died of an apparent blow to the face. Found in Dorseyville Cemetery by the caretaker.*" I didn't read anymore.

73

"Look, it's a way for us to find evidence against him. I don't think I'll be in any danger. Mrs. Glassport, Miss Talbot, and Mrs. Storkle sat for him and nothing happened to them."

"*Mrs. Storkle?* How do you know she sat for him?"

"Oh, okay. You were bound to find out sooner or later. I went to his studio last week when my dad had his tires rotated."

"You did *what?*"

"It was no big deal. I just wanted to see where his studio was, that's all. And it was right there, on the sixth floor, where the lady in the gallery said it was."

"Priggs, when are you going to get some sense in your head?"

"I *have* sense! It doesn't make sense to you because *you* didn't think of it first. You would have done the same thing if you were waiting for your dad across the street from the Landmark Apartments."

Art blew out the air from his cheeks. "What am I going to do with you?" His voice sounded exasperated, but his eyes were gentle. "So what did you find out?"

"Not much. Mrs. Storkle was there, posing for him. And Mr. Sanguine gave her a really hard time. You should have heard the way he talked to her!" I chuckled. "The door to his studio was open a little and I heard everything. He said something about a model to kill for."

"*A model to kill for?* Are you sure that's what he said?"

"Positive."

"Then what happened?"

"Nothing. A man came into the hallway, and I ran for the stairs."

"Did Sanguine see you?"

"No."

"Well, that's good. Now listen, if you're going to that studio, I'm going with you. No ifs, ands, or buts! Got that?"

"Why, Pini, I didn't know you cared so much about what happened to me!"

"You keep that up and you'll almost pass for a girl," he said, reaching out to rearrange my hair. "Almost, but not quite."

Later that afternoon, the four of us met up in Aspinwall to work on our project. Art, Fawn, and I had arrived by bus; Tucker had ridden into town with his mom, as usual. When we entered the public library, I noticed a familiar hum. Whispers added together created a buzz that covered up other whispers. Great if you wanted to talk; annoying if you wanted to read. We were here for both.

"Let's divide and conquer." Art spoke quietly with an authority he didn't have. "Tucker, you ask the librarian for help. Find anything you can on Captain Bridgeway. Fawn, you take notes. Scratch that. Priggs, you take notes. Fawn, you sit here and look pretty. I'll check the Internet."

Fawn straightened up, grinned, and tossed back her hair.

"Why does Fawn get to look pretty?" I asked.

"Everyone's got a job to do. That happens to be the one she does best. I would let you do it, Priggs, but you have a zit on your nose."

I covered my nose with my hand and said, "Come on, Tucker, we don't have all night."

Forty minutes later, we returned to the table. "What did you find?" Art asked.

Fawn proudly pulled the folded sheet of brown paper from her backpack and unfolded it. "The rubbing of Captain Andrew Bridgeway's headstone. I did my part."

Tucker handed me the note cards. I started to go over what we had found: "Captain Bridgeway fought gallantly alongside his men at the battle of Vicksburg—"

"Who's going to type the report?" Fawn interrupted.

"I will," Art offered. "Tucker and I can put it together, right?"

Tucker nodded.

"Okay, then we're done for tonight." I handed him the stack of cards.

"I have to call my dad," Tucker whispered.

"You don't have to," Fawn said. "My dad could give you a ride home."

"No, I have to call him," he said softly, pulling his cell phone out of the pocket of his preppy green jacket.

"Okay, we'll wait for you outside."

Mr. Riggoli drove up to the curb in a car with no rust, no door dings, and no splatted bugs on the windshield. It was a new Jaguar in a shade of gray-green my mother called the color of old money. Tucker's dad looked polished as always, as if he dressed to fit the car.

We all knew Tucker was expected to fit into his dad's suits someday, but it was hard to believe by looking at him tonight. Waiting by the curb, Tucker appeared meek, almost frightened. It wasn't that Mr. Riggoli meant to scare the pants off Tucker; he just was bigger, smarter, and better than most people, which made it unthinkable that Tucker could ever win any race against his dad.

I nudged Tucker to remind him to ask his dad about the purse, but he said nothing.

It was Art who spoke up when the window had rolled down. "Hi, Mr. Riggoli."

"Hi, Art," Tucker's dad called. "Do you kids need a ride?"

"No, Fawn's dad will be here and he'll take us home," I said. *He would have taken Tucker home, too*, I thought, but what was the point in saying it? Tucker never rode home with anyone other than his parents.

"Okay."

Tucker hopped into the front seat on the passenger side as Mr. Riggoli pulled in his arm.

Art yelled into the opening as the electric window started to close. "We want to ask you something, It's about the woman who was murdered."

"Whoa!" The window went back down. "Before you say anymore, you should know that I'm an accountant for the city. I work at the Police Station, but I'm not a police officer. I don't have anything to do with investigations. And if I did, I couldn't talk about it, could I?"

"No, you couldn't," Art said.

I nodded my head in understanding. "I guess there isn't accounting work involved in a murder."

"Oh, you'd be surprised. All of the evidence—clothing, jewelry, anything found at the crime scene—has to be put into inventory. We keep precise logs, everything by the book."

Fawn perked up. "Wow! Then you saw those red shoes. Weren't they something?"

Mr. Riggoli put up his hand to stop her from saying anymore. His voice took on an official tone. "I know the four of you saw the first murder victim, but like I said—"

"There's just one thing puzzling me," I broke in. "The *Herald* said the second murder victim was found with a beaded purse. Was there one lion clasp on that purse or two?"

"Did the *Herald* say there were two clasps?" Mr. Riggoli asked. He continued to speak, more to himself than to us. "I inventoried that purse myself and I'm positive there was just one." I could almost hear the powerful wireless computer in his head researching his fact- and number-filled database. "A female lion's head—yes, I'm sure there was only one."

"Well," Art replied. "You can't talk about it and we shouldn't ask you any questions."

"That's right, son," he nodded with a satisfied look that we had the proper respect for authority.

I smiled. Art and I were getting good at this.

Would you like me to wait here until your dad arrives?" Mr.

Riggoli asked Fawn.

"No, that's okay," she said, Her eyes were downcast.

I knew she was disappointed that she couldn't ask him more about the red shoes. It would have been the high point of her night.

As the taillights of the Jaguar disappeared from view, Art came up behind me. "Slick. Very slick. I couldn't have done better myself."

I deliberately raised my eyebrows and tipped up my chin as if to say, "No kidding?"

Chapter 18: Layers Revealed

On Monday afternoon, I had a free period and decided to go to the computer lab. I took a seat in the back of the room as far away from a group of boys as I could get. You just never know with them; they let loose body noises and worse without warning.

I logged on, entered my student password and typed "Askjeeves.com." The all-knowing wizard of the web appeared like a butler wearing a black suit, white shirt, and red tie. In the search field, I typed "A-l-e-x-a-n-d-e-r B-r-i-d-g-e-w-a-y" and hit the enter key. A listing appeared for "Civil War Trivia of the Month: Olivia Lindsey and Alexander Bridgeway."

I double-clicked on the link and read the account:

> As the Civil War escalated in July of 1862, President Abraham Lincoln sent out a call for an additional 300,000 men to serve in the Union Army. Although not a man, 19-year-old Olivia Lindsey was eager to join. She dressed in men's clothing and volunteered for military service.

Alexander...*a girl?* I pictured this beautiful, young Victorian woman, with waist-length hair tucked up under a cap, dressed in suspenders and work boots, marching into the recruiting office. I imagined her speaking in her lowest voice when she belted out the words, "I'm here to enlist." *Surely, she would be found out.* I read on:

> Olivia Lindsey was transformed into Alexander (Alex) Bridgeway, younger brother of Captain Andrew Bridgeway, but in truth, Captain Bridgeway was Olivia's fiancé. She enlisted to be with him.
>
> Reading and writing were not required of volunteers (Olivia could do neither). She marked an "X" on the enlistment papers and passed the preinduction physical examination, which involved just a quick look in the eyes and ears.

Ahhhh . . . that was it! Love...it made her crazy. Love can do that to a girl. Not that I had any first-hand knowledge of that subject, but I'd read about it.

> After a month spent in basic training, the troops received orders to leave for Columbus, Kentucky, to

serve under Ulysses S. Grant. Over the next three years, the 95th traveled 9,000 miles across Dixie soil, taking part in the bloody siege at Vicksburg. In the heat of battle, Alexander was captured by rebels. He reportedly "seized a gun from the guard, knocked down the man and fled back to the Union camp."

Olivia/Alex managed to survive the war without arousing suspicion as to her true sexual identity. Some accounts by fellow comrades indicate that the other soldiers just assumed Alex was shy: "He was of very retiring disposition and did not take part in any games. He had very small hands and feet. He was the smallest man in the company." In return for assistance in tasks involving heavy lifting, Alexander would sew on buttons and mend torn clothing.

In 1864, Captain Andrew Bridgeway was wounded in battle and died.

Her fiancé died in battle! Oh, how sad. After all she had done. It was too tragic to think about. *What happened to her?*

Olivia continued to serve until the 95th Pennsylvania Infantry Volunteers were finally discharged in August of 1865. She moved to Dorseyville, Pennsylvania, and continued life as a man, still posing as the brother of the late Andrew Bridgeway.

When the little soldier died on October 10, 1915, her true identity was discovered by the undertaker. Olivia/Alex was dressed in uniform. The casket was draped with the American flag, With full military honors, Olivia/Alex was buried in Pine Creek Presbyterian Cemetery in Dorseyville, Pennsylvania, next to the only man she had ever loved, Captain Andrew

Bridgeway. The grave is marked with a plain tomb-stone, simply inscribed, "Alexander Bridgeway, Co. 6, 95th PA Inf.

Why did she continue to dress like a man? Maybe she loved him so much, she vowed to never marry anyone else. Perhaps that's why she hid her femininity. The article didn't say.

I printed out the information. *It wouldn't hurt if I typed up a report on Olivia—or Alex—for extra credit, would it?*

The halls were deserted when I finished. I juggled three books under one arm, balanced my backpack on one knee that I propped up on the locker below mine, and slid my pencil between my teeth so I could have a hand free to yank out my gym clothes that were wedged under a tower of books, papers, and an emergency can of soda.

Tucker appeared down the hall wearing his soccer uniform. He broke up as he soon as he saw me.

I raised my eyebrows and released my pencil from my teeth, letting it fall to the floor. "Oh, you think this is funny?"

"Noooo," he said, dragging the word out as if he had more to say. He broke up laughing again, trying to cover his mouth with his hand.

"Then what's so funny?"

"The locker room...," he said softly. Before he could finish, a new wave of laughter came over him.

"*What?*"

"Art got you good," Tucker whispered between chuckles.
I dropped my books, my backpack, and my gym clothes. If I wanted to talk to Tucker, I would have to give him my full attention. I put my hands on my hips. Already, I suspected I was not going to like this. With a stance that blocked his escape, I asked, "What about the locker room?"

"I can't say." He did a little dance and cracked up again.

I had never seen Tucker this loose. I grabbed his shoulders and brought him back to his full upright and locked position. "*What? What, Tucker? What* did Art say about me?"

He squeezed his lips together, trying hard to hold back the giggles. His exaggerated smiley face was about to explode. "He said you were flat." It came out in a whisper that rolled into a swell of laughter…a typical guy kind of laughter.

I slugged him...*hard*...in his upper arm. I picked up my books, my pencil, my backpack, my gym clothes, and my dignity. Slamming the locker door, I turned my back on him. Then I cussed.

ℭhapter 19: On my Own

From then on, I avoided Art. Wherever he was, I wasn't. I pretended I couldn't see him, even if he called my name.

When Saturday morning arrived, I awoke early and boarded the 8:20 bus to Aspinwall. It was no accident that Art wasn't with me. I didn't need him to go with me to the artist's studio. I didn't need him on the same planet with me.

I walked quickly to the Landmark Apartments, pacing myself as I half-ran, half-walked up the stairs. All the way up, I told myself I had nothing to worry about. *Mrs. Glassport, Mrs. Talbot, and Mrs. Storkle had been here and nothing had happened to them.* With an unsteady hand, I knocked on the partially open door to apartment 602.

"Come in," Mr. Sanguine spoke in a hearty, but not entirely welcoming voice.

I entered his world with slow steps, not sure what to expect. The large room unfolded in astounding splashes of color. Pastel, watercolor, and oil paintings rested on the floor, leaning like beauty contestant finalists along the back wall. The room had a faint smell of Crayolas mixed with my mom's furniture polishing rags. A wooden counter to the right of the entrance was filled with art supplies. I longed to touch them, to feel their power in my hand. The only sign that Mr. Sanguine lived here was the twin bed in the corner, next to the nearly floor-to-ceiling windows.

"Come over here," he said. "Don't be shy."

He was wearing a once-white apron, the kind a cook might wear, with splashes of reds and blues and purples on it; a black streak slashed across the top of the apron over the place where his heart might be. I approached with caution, remembering the red shoes and the beaded purse. I gulped.

"Nervous about art? Why is that?" he asked, handing me a brush. "Where there is fear, there is no creativity! You must ap-proach your art with the confidence of a god. The secret to that confidence," he said, as if he thought me worthy of hearing his secrets, "is *not* that we artists don't make mistakes. We *do*—all the time! The difference between the true artist and the amateur is that the artist knows how to fix them. We are not afraid to turn our mistakes into something beautiful!"

To my surprise, he winked.

He proceeded to give me my first lesson in the many ways to hold the brush: in between my fingers, like a drawing tool; in my fist, like a weapon; as an extension of my arm to create broad, sweeping strokes; close to the end of the metal bar like a razor to scrape the surface; and upside down, using the pointed end to etch lines into the paper.

Before I knew it, the first hour was up.

"Now it's my turn," he said. "Be seated in the chair, there, next to the window."

I had no idea how to "be seated" in the chair. I sat down as if I were in church—two feet flat on the floor, my back straight, and my hands folded in my lap.

He laughed and said, "Here, let me pose you."

His eyes seemed to grow darker as his face neared mine. His hand almost touched my shoulder. I shivered.

"Are you cold?" he asked.

"No. I mean, I've never modeled before," I said, thinking again of Art and how he said I shouldn't come here alone. I gripped the arms of the chair with determination.

"Look to the right. Chin down a little, eyes up." He gestured for me to move my shoulder, first down, then back. When he was satisfied with my pose, he turned and walked over to his work area, picked up a pencil, and began to sketch.

I watched the clock on the wall. Mr. Sanguine said nothing to me. He worked with such a depth of intensity that he seemed to be somewhere else. A few times, he muttered to himself about the light, the tone of my skin, or the color of my hair. After twenty minutes, he stepped away from his work. He spoke to me. "Let's take a break now. Have a pop."

Is this where he drugs me, murders me, and then paints something I own? Like what? I don't own anything as eye-catching as the red shoes or the purse. Or will he paint me with something I don't own?

He reached into a small refrigerator under the counter, took out a soda, and handed it to me.

Examining the can for signs of tampering and not finding any, I popped the top. The seal broke, releasing a fizzing sound. *Good. The vacuum hasn't been broken by a hypodermic needle.* Otherwise, the soda would have been flat, I reasoned. I took a drink. It tasted normal.

"I have to empty this and get clean water." He picked up the small, white bucket. "I'll be back." He went through a doorway that led to another room, and the door closed behind him.

I ran over to see his painting of me. *How did I look to him?* It was only a rough shape of a seated person without details. Disappointed, I put the can on the counter. Casually, I moseyed around the room, gazing at the paintings, so that if he came back and saw me, perhaps it would look like I was merely interested in his work. I walked over to the window and looked out. Perched on a hanging platform on the other wing of the building, directly across from me, was a man washing windows. I looked closer. I could see a woman standing in the window of an apartment one floor below, watching him. She was dressed in a prim gray pantsuit. Hadn't I seen her before? Then it hit me: *The woman who worked in the art gallery—the one who had told me to stay away from Mr. Sanguine! Coincidence? Is there a connection between the artist, the gallery woman, and the murders?*

I moved around the room, checking out every surface looking for clues. On a desk in the corner, a light blue invitation with silver letters caught my eye:

The Aspinwall Art Gallery
Invites You to Attend
The Artist's Reception
and Premier Exhibition of Fine Art
by Renowned Local Artist

Eduardo Sanguine

I scanned the invitation for the date and time. *This Saturday at 3 p.m.! Interesting. Will there be any new paintings on display...with more items from recently murdered women? Maybe he'll display the painting of me....* I gave my brain a shake. *Don't go there. There's no time to waste.*

I scanned the room. *What kind of clues would the dead women leave behind?* I racked my brain trying to remember. Atalia Trinski wasn't wearing a coat when we found her. Could her coat be here? Where?

I knelt down, lowered my face to the floor, and looked under the bed. *Dust bunnies, yes; coat, no. Humph.* My eyes were drawn to the closet door. I glanced back at the door where Mr. Sanguine had disappeared. *Do I dare?*

I sauntered over to the mystery door. I paused and looked back again. I placed my hand around the brass knob. I held my breath, turning the knob ever so slowly. *Thank you, God.* It wasn't locked.

Chapter 20: Mortally Wounded

"Don't touch that door!" Mr. Sanguine bellowed in a deep tone I hadn't heard from him before.

I froze. *Where had* he *come from?* My heart raced, as blood rushed to my cheeks.

"*What are you doing?*" he yelled. "Snooping?"

"No, I'm sorry," I stammered. "I was just curious about your paintings. I wondered if you had any more in there."

"Whether I *do* or whether I *don't*, it's none of *your* business. I won't have you here if I can't trust you—*do you understand?*"

I nodded, too scared to speak.

"Now take your seat. We don't have much time."

Much time, I repeated to myself. *Much time for what? Much time for me to live?*

91

The second he returned to his painting, his mood changed. His eyes looked glazed and remote. Once again, he seemed to retreat to a place so far removed from this galaxy that I could only wonder where he went while he painted. Was it a dark and brooding prison or a palace filled with color and light?

At exactly eleven o'clock, he put down his brush. "That's all for today," he said.

I picked up my backpack and turned to leave.

"Priggs—is that your nickname?" he asked.

I nodded.

"You have raw talent. More importantly, you have curiosity and guts. If you are willing to do the work and are determined to learn, you might someday become an artist."

I studied his face. He looked neither sinister nor repelling. As my opinion softened, I smiled at him. "Thank you, Mr. Sanguine. I'll see you next Saturday."

Chapter 21: Revenge!

"I'll never speak to Art again as long as I live!" I said, punching Fawn's pink pillow for effect.

"That's the way!" Fawn exclaimed, sympathetically.

"He and his stupid locker room buddies. He thinks he's a jock around them."

"Yeah."

"Boobs aren't the only thing," I rationalized, flopping over on her bed.

"They aren't?" Fawn asked.

"No. We're women with brains!"

"Speak for yourself."

"Well, you're a woman of fashion and that's just as good."

93

"But with boobs, would we need brains or fashion?"

"What are you saying? What can boobs do for us? Look at Darlene Lipinski. She has boobs. Have you seen how she combs her hair and puts on makeup in the locker room wearing only a bra?"

Fawn laughed, nodding. "Well, don't go off the deep end. If we should happen to wake up one morning blessed with voluptuous bosoms, we'll figure out what to do with them. Keep an open mind."

"Until that day comes, I don't want Art making fun of me."

"I don't blame you."

"Do I make fun of him for being short?"

"*Yes!*"

I laughed.

"Priggs, what about our team project and our plans to find the murderer? How are we gonna work together if you aren't talking to Art?"

"That's his problem. He should have thought of that before he said I was flat."

"Ohhhh-kay. If you don't care about your grade…." Fawn's voice trailed off as she shrugged her shoulders.

"Oh, don't worry. Art will type the report and hand it in. He and Tucker want a good grade, so they'll work hard on it. As for solving the murder, I just might solve it on my own. You can tell Art from me that I don't need his help."

"Maybe he likes you," Fawn said.

She often surprised me with her understanding of people. It was a skill I didn't possess. "Oh, really?"

"Really!" she said.

"How do you figure?"

"Maybe he just doesn't want any other boys to like you. Have you thought of that?"

"If he likes me, he could find a better way to show it."

"He's been hitting you over the head for nine years. Now he's in a new phase."

"What phase is that?"

"It's the 'challenging your femininity to get your attention' phase."

"*What?*"

"*Yes!* You need to show him that you can be irresistible to any boy. It will drive him insane."

"He already is!"

"Look here, in *Teen Scene* magazine…." She reached for it on the top of a stack of magazines on her nightstand. 'Dos and Don'ts of Fashion.' Now which one are you?"

I looked in the mirror. Ponytail, sweatshirt with holes you could slip a bunny through, grubby jeans, and mismatched socks. "Don't."

"Exactly!"

"Let me try something with your hair." She motioned for me to turn around. She swept my hair up and smoothed the sides back with her hands. "Fabulous. Now take a look. See how pretty it looks? You could be gorgeous!"

I gazed in the mirror over her dresser. It *was* an improvement, but I feared if I gave her the least little bit of encouragement, she would enthusiastically whip out hairspray, makeup, hair depilitators, and who knows what other products she had, and she would happily overwhelm me with a full-blown makeover. "Look, Fawn, I know you mean well," I said, shaking my hair loose, "but I don't want to attract any boy and I definitely don't want to attract *him*! Never did, don't now, never will. End of subject!"

Chapter 22: Sharing a Secret

The next morning, everything went wrong. Even though I tried my best to avoid my mother, I failed. At the end of an ugly encounter, my mother's words sliced through my skin.

"Heaven knows why I do anything for such an ungrateful, worthless, smart-mouthed kid...."

I grabbed my backpack and ran out of the kitchen. I could feel the heat rising in my cheeks as I closed the door behind me, cutting off my mother's words. It was still dark outside. It wouldn't be daylight for another half an hour. The cold turned sprinkling rain into a spit of snow flurries. I bent my head and began walking.

97

Today, I didn't mind the weather at all.

"Does she go off on you like that often?"

Art's voice surprised me. I closed my eyes and kept walking, hoping that when I opened them, he wouldn't be there.

But he was. He matched his steps to mine.

"I came by to see if I could walk you to the bus stop. I saw your mother yelling at you through the window." His shoulder bumped mine as we walked along the edge of the road where the asphalt met the gravel. A thin layer of brittle ice crunched under our feet.

I pulled the hood of my parka down lower on my forehead to hide my face and moved away from him. "It was nothing."

He stopped walking and grasped the sleeve of my parka. He pulled me to the side of the road under the sheltering arms of an ancient pine tree. He turned towards me. He watched my face closely, watched me wince, watched the tears I could feel spilling down my cheeks, and saw my shame. I squeezed my eyes shut as tightly as I could.

"Priggs," he said in his deep, steady voice, "I won't let anyone hurt you—understand, kid?"

I nodded without opening my eyes. *Why didn't he go away? Didn't he know that we were uneven now?*

He put his hands on my shoulders and hugged me to his chest. "Let me know if this happens again, okay?"

I buried my head in his jacket. I would never ask him for help, just as I had never asked my father. Some things are given to you at birth, things you don't ask for and don't want. How could I explain that to him? Art had everything. I accepted the strange gifts of my birth—willfulness, curiosity, my right leg that was three-eighths of an inch longer than my left one, and my mother. I might not understand who she really was under her many moods and faces, but she was mine, and I accepted her.

"It's okay," I heard him say.

Slowly, my chest relaxed. My hood slid back on my head.

In my hair, he spoke softly, "I came to say I'm sorry."

That was the spark I needed. I pushed him away.

He quickly added, "I didn't say you were flat."

"Don't lie to me. Tucker said—"

"Concave." He smiled a very small smile. "I said you were cute but that your chest is concave."

I puffed out my chest. Looking down, I saw that there would be no boost to my argument there. I crossed my arms.

"All the guys were saying that they thought you were cute and they would like to get with you," he explained.

"They said that?" I asked.

"They did."

In spite of my anger, I smiled.

"Priggs, I meant it when I said you were cute; I was only kidding about you being flat."

I studied his face. He had been my friend for so long. I should have known he wouldn't turn on me. Oh, he might joke about me, but on another level, he would always stand beside me. He and

Fawn—the two people in my world who were really as they good as they seemed. Now Tucker...he just needed to be slugged once in a while.

"So am I forgiven?" he asked.

"Yes, but if you *ever* . . .

He raised his hand. "Buds?"

I slapped his hand.

"Come on," I said, not waiting for his reply, "we'll miss the bus." I ran, tasting the first new flakes of snow on my tongue and feeling freer than I had in a long time.

Chapter 23: The Countdown Begins

On Friday, we all met in the school library for second period study hall. Mrs. Povick, the library clerk, stood behind the information desk checking out books for a short line of kids. She was friendlier than Mrs. Storkle. With her in charge, we could get away with talking, as long as we weren't too loud.

"You said the reception starts at three?" Art asked me in a low voice.

"That's what it said on the invitation."

"Okay, let's meet in front of the gallery on Saturday at a quarter to three."

"What should we wear?" Fawn asked.

Art sighed and gave her a look he saved especially for dumb questions.

101

"*What?*" Fawn said in response to his look. "I've never been to an artist's reception before. It sounds like a formal affair. We don't want to show up in jeans and find out everyone's wearing evening gowns and tuxedos, do we?"

"You're right. No jeans. Maybe a dress would be better," I said.

Fawn turned to the guys. "Could you two try to look sophisticated?"

Art gave her a smirk.

"At least take a bath, okay?"

"Could we *please* get back to our plans?" Art asked. Without pausing, he continued, "Do you think all of the paintings will be there?"

"I don't know. The flyer said it would be an exhibit of his recent works."

"If the paintings *are* there, then we'll call the police and show them the clues," he replied.

"Is there enough proof for the police to arrest him?" Tucker asked.

"That's a good question," Fawn answered.

It was a question that never left my mind as I sat through my afternoon classes. *Did the red shoes and the beaded purse with the two lions' head clasps make Sanguine a murderer? What did I really know about him? He barked at Mrs. Storkle. And he talked about "a model to kill for." Who did he mean? Mrs. Storkle? The murdered women? Had they modeled for him?*

Did he have paintings of them? If so, where were they? Maybe in his closet. That would explain why he screamed at me when he caught me trying to open the door. But why would he want to kill those actresses? Okay, he hated people, he was eccentric, but did that make him a murderer?

When we talked about art, when he was teaching me, I almost liked him. He was a different person when he was painting. During those times, I had to keep reminding myself that he could be a murderer. I sighed. I couldn't figure it out.

Where could I find the answers? Maybe in his closet. My only opportunity would be tomorrow morning.

"Mr. Sanguine," I asked as innocently as I knew how the next morning, "can you tell me about the painting you did of Mrs. Glassport?"

"Oh, you saw it?" he asked. His eyes never left his palette.

"I saw it in the window of the art gallery on the way to the library a few weeks ago."

"It's still in the gallery. My one-man show opens there this afternoon."

"It must be exciting to have a one-man show," I said without moving.

"Exciting?" This time he did look up. "You think it's exciting to have to talk to a bunch of small town wanna-be art critics? It's excruciating, that's what it is. I loathe receptions."

"Then why do you do it?" I asked.

His eyes went back to his painting. "In the hopes that someday I'll be discovered by someone in a bigger city, someone who matters in the art community."

I held my tongue but thought: *What were the odds that someone from New York or Paris would be in Aspinwall tonight?*

He read my mind. "Oh, big city critics won't be at the reception today, but the newspaper, radio, and TV cultural art reporters will be. If they cover my work, I might get national exposure. That's why I do it."

"That makes sense." I paused. "Can you tell me about the painting you did of Mrs. Glassport?"

"What can I tell you? She's one of the most obnoxious people I have ever endured. It would have been intolerable if not for the shoes. Did you like them?"

I froze.

He looked up from his work, piercing my eyes with his.

A chill ran down my spine like the knife down the back of a fryer before the butcher hacks it into pieces for fried chicken. I couldn't come up with an answer. "Ahhh...."

A phone rang in the distance. Mr. Sanguine dried his hands on his apron. "Take a break while I get the phone. Maybe it's the press."

As soon as he disappeared into the other room and the door closed behind him, I bolted off my chair, dashed to the closet door and, without hesitation, opened the door.

The light from the windows streamed into the darkness. The air in the storeroom escaped with a sickly smell of mustiness. Paintings lined the floor on either side of the closet. Only a small space for walking remained in the middle. I wasn't sure what I was looking for. *What* did *the dead women look like? The woman in the tree had a mangled face. Even though the Herald showed a photo of her on stage, her face had been small and hard to see. And I never saw a photo of the second woman*

I moved through the narrow space, carefully tilting each of the ornate frames to see the paintings behind. Each one contained a portrait of the same woman, someone who looked magnificent, elegantly dressed, with beautiful jewelry, furs, or purses.

I looked through the last stack. *Well, that answers that. It doesn't matter what the dead women looked like. They aren't in these paintings, and I don't see any dead bodies here.*

I backed out of the closet and looked around. I exhaled. Mr. Sanguine was still in the other room. I shut the door as quietly as I could. For once, luck was on my side.

When Mr. Sanguine returned, I was posed in the antique chair reading *Pride and Prejudice*, trying to look like the picture of a meek and innocent girl.

At eleven a.m. sharp, I ran down the stairs, out of the Landmark Apartment building, and into the welcome sunshine. Stepping over each crack in the sidewalk on the way to the J & W Variety Store, my thoughts played ping-pong with the facts. *The first woman's body was found in Pine Creek Cemetery, the second in Dorseyville Cemetery.*

Was there a reason the murderer left the women in a cemetery? Atalia Trinski had been carefully placed in that tree. Almost like a stage set up, as if it had been put there for show. Was the second woman found in a similar setting? There was no way to find that out and Mr. Riggoli would never tell me.

What about the third woman? How do I know there even is a third woman? The earrings might be a clue. Mrs. Storkle would never wear such dangly jewelry. But if there was a third dead woman, where was she? In another cemetery? There was one more cemetery in the area. We had found it while doing research on Civil War burial sites. *If a body had been dumped there, wouldn't it have been found by now? Maybe not; the place is pretty remote. There's only one way to find out,* I thought as I reached my destination.

The J & W Variety Store had supplied candy and ice cream bars to Fawn and me as far back as I could remember—school binders and notebook paper when we learned to write; lots of last-minute gifts for our moms on Valentine's Day and Mother's Day. I still liked the smell of the place—mango-scented candles and cheap, plastic bowls.

Fawn was standing outside next to a sign in the window that said 'Gordy's Original Beef Jerky, 50 cents.' My dad loved that stuff, but I wasn't here for beef jerky; I was here to meet Fawn and buy postage stamps for my mom.

"*There* you are," Fawn said when she saw me, opening the door for me. "I was worried about you. I hate to think of you in that creepy guy's studio by yourself."

"He's not always creepy," I replied.

Fawn followed me to the back of the store where three people stood in line. On the wall next to a small U.S. flag was an official-looking sign that said 'U.S. Post Office,' right above the vacuum cleaner bags.

"He answered the phone and, while he was in the other room, I searched his closet."

Her eyes opened wide.

"Relax. No dead bodies."

The man ahead of us turned suddenly to look at me. His dark, curly hair and piercing blue eyes looked familiar. Where had I seen him before? *Maybe he looks like someone on TV.* Just as quickly, he snapped back around.

"Just a bunch of paintings."

"Well, it doesn't matter," Fawn said. "Art says he'll be caught tonight. After you get your mom's stamps, can you come home with me and help me pick out something to wear?"

"Sure. Can I borrow something from you?" I asked, stepping up to the counter.

She elbowed me. "Of course."

"A book of stamps, please," I said to the man with the U.S. Post Office nametag. He gave me the stamps. I paid him with the money my mom had given me, then Fawn and I walked single file up the narrow aisle to the door. We waved to Miss Talbot as we passed the checkout counter.

"The river should have crested by now," I heard Mrs. Borland saying to her, "but instead, it keeps getting higher and higher. I don't understand it."

"I'll call my mom and ask if I can go to the reception straight from your house," I said, grabbing Fawn's arm. "That way, we can get dressed and go together, okay?"

"Good idea," Fawn said.

I wondered if she was listening to me or if her brain was already a million miles away, planning our entrance into high society.

The curly-haired man stood on the sidewalk smoking a cigarette as we headed for the bus stop on the corner. I noticed his white pants, the kind that painters wear. I felt the hairs on my neck stand up, but I didn't know why.

Chapter 24: The Artist's Reception

Promptly at five o'clock, Mrs. Kendell, the gallery administrator, opened the doors and began welcoming a stream of guests into the anteroom. She had somehow been transformed from a serious guard of Aspinwall's most prized artwork into a warm and gracious hostess.

In spite of Fawn's close attention to our clothes, hair, and jewelry, no one noticed us in the tightly packed crowd. Above a group of short women, I caught sight of Art and Tucker. Their heads appeared to be clean and presentable. Anyone who didn't know them might mistakenly think they were handsome.

Fawn led me inside, where we found the coat room and dropped off our jackets and my backpack. Returning to the main gallery, we looked around the room. Eduardo Sanguine stood alone to one side of the crowd looking like the original that he was. Instead of a suit, he was wearing a soft, expensive-looking, black turtleneck; crisp, black, tailored pants; and imported, Italian leather shoes. It was Fawn who pointed out the details of his attire to me.

More people arrived, trapping Mr. Sanguine on all sides. Gushing matrons, some sandwiched into unflattering outfits, others stuffed into jungle-feverish floral dresses, and men strutting around pompously in off-the-rack suits and unimaginative print ties surrounded him. He visibly squirmed, trying to escape them.

I overheard Mrs. Glassport's loud cackle above the din.

"Mr. Sanguine? *Oh, there you are!* I've been looking for you."

Fawn and I smothered a giggle as she corralled the group like a herd of buffalo and wedged her way through the fray.

"This is my friend, Adelia Pennycamp. When I told her we were acquainted, she in*sisted* I bring her over and introduce you. She would like your autograph."

She turned to her friend, whose purple woven hat was slightly askew on her head. Its pink feathers had become more ruffled as a result of being yanked through the jostling crowd. Mrs. Glassport paused to catch her breath, smoothing the stretchy blue velvet fabric of her dress over her protruding hindquarters. "Mr. Sanguine, this is Mrs. Pennycamp. Adelia, *this* is the artist who painted me."

"I'm charmed to meet you," Mrs. Pennycamp gushed.

To Mrs. Glassport's disappointment, Mr. Sanguine mumbled, "Excuse me. I need air."

"What did he say?" Mrs. Pennycamp asked.

"He said he loves my hair," Mrs. Glassport replied over the noise of the crowd.

We ducked behind an easel so she wouldn't see us laughing. Art and Tucker found us there.

Tucker whispered, "Wow, you two look so grown up!"

Art gave a soft whistle. "Fawn, you always look pretty but I must say you outdid yourself this time. And Priggs—"

I held my breath.

"Look at you! You have legs!" His gaze swept over my outfit of Fawn's clothes and shoes. He walked around me in a wide circle. "You look like a princess." He looked like he had never seen me before.

Fawn nodded with an "I'm totally satisfied" expression on her face.

In spite of my desire not to blush, I felt my cheeks growing warm. "Yeah, you and Tucker look handsome, too. Now don't we have work to do?"

According to our plan, we split up in pairs—boys versus girls—to check out the paintings on either side of the room for new clues. Fawn walked confidently to the first display wall, as if this type of affair was nothing new to her. I did my best to do the same. My toes ached in her black satin shoes, but I sucked in the pain and glided with my hips leading the way, the way Fawn had taught me.

Mrs. Storkle's high-pitched voice bounced off the white-washed walls to the cathedral ceiling and back. "Trash, pure trash! I have never worn such jewelry. Those are the earrings of a harlot!"

Mrs. Povick, the library clerk standing next to her, tried her best to calm her down. "I got you earrings like those for Christmas, don't you remember?"

"You've never seen me wearing them, have you? That's because I'm a woman of refined taste. I wear only pure gold earrings, never costume imitations."

"Yes, I know," the clerk said, trying to get Mrs. Storkle to lower her voice. "And you have a beautiful collection of jewels from the Television Shopping Network."

Across the room, Miss Talbot, the one-armed woman, looked up at a painting of herself. Fawn and I eased in behind her.

"What do you think of the painting?" the woman beside her asked.

"Why, I am overwhelmed by it. He's so talented. I can't believe that's me in the painting. And you can see only my good side."

The other woman hesitated. "Aren't you offended by those lion head clasps?"

"He didn't live here when I lost my arm. He moved here years after it happened. He doesn't know."

Humbling, that's what it was to watch her as she gazed in awe at the beautiful portrait of herself. We made our way around the room until we met up with Art and Tucker.

"Well?" I asked. "Find anything?"

"The proof is all here," Art replied.

Chapter 25: Prove It!

"I'm not so sure," I said. "The only evidence we have is the red shoes and the purse. The earrings aren't proof because they aren't connected to a dead body."

Art let out an exasperated sigh. "Good heavens, Priggs! How much proof do you need?"

"Something doesn't fit. I can't put my finger on it."

"I say we call the police now," he argued.

"We just got here. Have some punch. There's a good spread of eats. I want to think about this."

"How long do you want us to wait?" Art asked.

I knew he was trying to pin me down, but I didn't know how much time I needed. "The reception isn't over until six." I checked my watch. "It's now 3:34. Wait until 5:00 to make the call, okay?"

113

I signaled to Fawn with my eyes. "Would you like to go with me to the girl's room?"

She turned to follow me.

"Honestly, why do we have to wait—" Art muttered behind us.

"Go eat! We'll be right back," I called to him.

When the bathroom door closed behind us, Fawn said, "Priggs, what's going on?"

"Shhhh!" Crouching down, I looked under the stalls for feet. "Okay, we're alone."

"So what's up?"

"Wait here. I'll be right back," I answered, running out the same door we had just come in. Less than a minute later, I returned to the bathroom carrying my backpack and raced to the handicapped stall. Fawn followed me in. I sighed as I stepped out of her killer shoes, then slipped off her most expensive black skirt with the dangly chain belt.

"What are you doing?" Fawn asked in amazement.

"Gotta change. Hand me my khakis."

She swooped up my backpack and clutched it to her chest. "I will not! This is the biggest night of our lives and you are *not* going out there in khakis!"

"Exactly," I said, grabbing the backpack. "I am not going out there. I'm going to catch a bus."

Her mouth fell open as I wiggled into my pants. Then I dropped to the ground to put on my hiking boots.

"And just where might *we* be going on the bus?"

"*We* aren't going. *I'm* going—to Crestwood Cemetery."

"You're kidding, right?" Her body became rigid as she assumed a firm stance. She had a look on her face I had never seen before—straight-jacket orderly or female prison guard—I didn't know which.

"No, I'm not kidding. I've been thinking about the murders. The first two women were found in cemeteries, right?" I pulled my sweatshirt out of the bag. "Mind if I wear this over your blouse?"

"Don't get it dirty."

"I won't. The first two women were found in different cemeteries, right?"

"Uh-huh."

I stood up, carefully folding her skirt and gently placing it in the bag over the tops of her shoes. "Well, I suspect there's a third dead woman's body in another cemetery and the only other cemetery in Dorseyville is Crestwood."

"She could be in a cemetery somewhere else, maybe in Aspinwall."

"Aspinwall doesn't have a cemetery."

"Oh. Don't you think the police would have looked in Crestwood already?"

"Maybe. But I want to take a look."

"Why? What difference will it make? We already have a plan to catch Sanguine."

"Because if she's there, and *if* she's wearing the *same* earrings

I saw him paint on Mrs. Storkle, then it will *prove* he's the murderer. It *proves* he saw the earrings even before the body was found."

"You want to prove to Art that you're smarter than him, don't you?"

"Than *he*." I corrected her. "And I already know I'm smarter." I zipped up the main compartment and turned to go. My voice grew softer. "Something's bothering me about Sanguine. I have to do this before we call the police."

"Priggs, you can't go to that cemetery alone."

"Look, you go out and dazzle Art and Tucker with your charm." She smirked.

I smiled and squeezed her arm with affection. "Okay, eat. Do anything to keep them busy. It won't take me more than an hour to hop on the bus, go to the cemetery, check it out, and get back to the gallery. I should be back before five." I gently pushed her towards the door. "Then I'll come back here and change into my gorgeous self."

"I don't think you —"

"Please, just stall them for an hour."

"Let me go with you." Her eyes were pleading. "You might be in danger."

"I won't be in any danger, unless you count the heart attack I'll have if I *do* see a dead body."

"I don't like this." Worry lines appeared on her forehead.

As much as I wished I could take her along, I couldn't risk

getting her into anymore trouble. I knew she would go with me without question if I gave her as much as a nod. She had always trusted me to be smart one, to steer us in the right direction. But this time, I had no compass; I'd have to go alone. My heart made me pause. I looked at her worried face. Fawn was everything to me. I turned quickly and lowered my head to hide my watering eyes.

I forced my voice to sound calm as I tried to reassure her, "Mr. Sanguine won't be there. He's here, remember? If you want to, you can keep an eye on him, okay? Wait for me. And don't tell Art and Tucker where I am." I gave her a quick hug. "I'll be back." I nudged her out the door. Slinging my backpack over my shoulder, I slipped out the front entrance.

At the bus stop, I pulled the hood of my jacket up over my head. In no time, the No. 7 Dorseyville Express was screeching to a stop in front of me. Jumping up the steps, I quickly dropped the coins into the box, all the while keeping my head down. I found a seat near the back, although almost all of seats were empty.

As the bus picked up speed, my mind raced, already on high alert. *What will I need? Gloves.* I pulled them out of the side pocket of my backpack and put them in my coat pocket. *A flashlight.* I found the small one I always carried to walk home from Fawn's house and stuck it in my back pocket. *Nerves of steel. Darn. I wouldn't find that in my backpack.*

117

Chapter 26: Closing the Gap

The only remaining passenger, other than me, exited at the last bus stop in Aspinwall. The tires rumbled and spun on the loose gravel that filled the ruts in the road, causing the bus to hesitate, as if it could move only when I willed it to move. The tires finally grabbed the solid asphalt, and the bus lurched forward. *Funny. I hadn't decided to go forward. But that's life for you. Hop on a bus headed for a cemetery and you have no one to blame but yourself.*

Miles later, I made out some of the letters on the weathered sign for Crestwood Cemetery—the ones that weren't hidden by an overgrown pine branch. The sun hung low over the distant ridge. *There should be at least another hour and a half of daylight.*

Getting on the bus had been easy; getting off was going to take some courage. I pulled the cord.

The screeching sound of the brakes signaled the slowing of the tires. I struggled to stop my body as it pitched forward up the aisle. I grabbed the pole next to the driver and hung on.

"You want to get off here?" the balding driver asked.

I considered the question. When I didn't move, he waved a hand toward the door in a shooing motion.

I stood my ground. *You can't shoo me off this bus. I'll go when I'm ready.*

"This the stop you want? You rang the bell. Not many people ask me to stop at Crestwood," he said.

Still, I hesitated.

"Look, honey, you can get off here and dig up a date."

I looked at him and blinked.

He chuckled.

I turned my back on him as I descended the stairs. *Three, two, one, off the bus.* The door closed behind me with a squealing blast of air.

Weeds grew over the sprawling fields, up to the knees of the headstone guards. I glanced at my watch. Four o'clock. *A quick run-through, fifteen minutes, tops. Then I'll catch the next bus back to Aspinwall. I should have no problem getting back to the gallery before five.* Art's plan wasn't a bad one. It just needed one more thing to make it work perfectly—another dead body.

Chapter 27: Closer, Ever Closer

The uneven ground and the brittle weeds, thick and matted in spots, made it hard to hurry. I had to step carefully, moving slowly down each row. *At least the ground is firm. It would be the pits if it were muddy.*

Looking out over the field, I didn't see anything unusual. *Well, what did I expect? That a dead body would whistle and holler out, "Here I am"?* The body in the tree hadn't been visible from the road. *If there is a dead body here, I'll have to find it; it isn't going to find me.*

It seemed like it took forever to plod through the main part of the cemetery. I checked my watch. Time was playing tricks on me. *Only 10 minutes?* I counted headstones without bases, and bases without headstones, and even a few headstones overturned, but no body. *Was that good or bad?*

The smaller section off to the side was easier going. The stones were farther apart. From the dates, I guessed these were the old timers.

A wild turkey gobbled. I placed my hand over my heart as it began beating wildly, as if someone had jumped out from behind a headstone. My heart continued to pound like a boom box, even though I knew the noise was only a bird.

I tried to calm myself. *Get a grip. Only one more section down over that hill.* A stand of stick trees lined the edge of the graves at the far end. The leaves had fallen and gathered together like blown, tattered quilts, adding to the decay of the place.

"Grubbs, Patterson…." I called the names out as I passed by each of the weathered stones. Hearing my own voice, a human sound, relaxed me, or at least speaking aloud covered up the little noises of the field—noises of animals scurrying, wings flapping, and a million minute sounds that mark the beat of time in a timeless wilderness.

Maybe this is the witching hour—the hour between daylight and darkness. Nonsense! Just stuff in spooky books. These people are dead. There is nothing scary about this place. I haven't seen a body, I haven't dug up my date yet, and it's almost time to catch the bus back to meet Fawn.

Fawn. If she were here now, we would have been laughing about this by now.

"McDermott, Gamble...." My right foot didn't quite touch the ground. Something lunged out of the weeds and grasped my ankle. For a moment, I teetered. Something tightened around my leg and pulled me down. My head struck something—*HARD!*

Chapter 28: Trapped

I opened my eyes slowly. *Ohhhh. Ouch! What's that wet stuff on my face?* I wanted to get up, but couldn't. I looked down. Ropes circled around my chest and shoulders like a harness. My left arm was tied above the elbow but hung freely below.

Where am I? I realized I was sitting on the base of a headstone, my back pressed against freezing granite. My legs were crossed at the knees. My right arm was outstretched, resting on something icy cold. I turned to look. *A woman!* Dried blood covered her forehead as well as one eye. Her dangling, rhinestone earrings swayed from side to side.

"*Aaaaaahhhhhhh!!!!*" I screamed from my gut and squeezed my eyes shut. The tuna sandwich I had gulped down before leaving the gallery made its way up my throat. I coughed and sputtered. The contents of my stomach retched from my mouth. Pulling my arm away from her shoulder, I knew something was horribly wrong. She was...*DEAD!*

"Good evening," a man's voice called out as I wiped my face with the sleeve of my jacket.

The woman horrified me. *Don't look. Pretend she isn't there. Just think about what to do.* I tried to get a clear focus on him, the blurry figure standing in front of me. The light was fading and my eyes hurt. He was wearing white pants and, with the light from the sinking sun shining behind him, they glowed. The kind of pants painters wear, but there was no paint on them. He was leaning heavily on a metal baseball bat.

I struggled to speak. "Who are you?"

"Who you expecting? Your lover maybe? He raised a green glass bottle to his lips and took a swig. The bottle was almost empty.

"The artist."

"Oh, so that's who you planned to meet tonight, you shameless piece of filth. Is this your secret meeting place?"

What's going on? Who is this man—and who does he think I am? "I think there's some mistake. I was looking for a headstone for a class project."

"Shut up! Don't act with me! You never loved me." His words slurred. His body swayed slightly. "Do you think I'm a fool?" He raised the baseball bat in a wild gesture. A halo of light flashed over his dark, curly hair. The top part of his body waved from side-to-side like the mast of a sailboat swaying against the murky, reddish sky. The wind shifted. The smell of liquor carried on the breeze to my nose.

He's...the man at the Post Office! "Wait!" I pleaded with him. "You were standing in front of me in the J & W Variety Store this afternoon. Don't you remember me?"

His angry expression turned to one of confusion. He cocked his head to one side, as if listening to voices I couldn't hear.

"You're one of those no-good actresses."

"No, I was buying stamps. Remember?"

"Nooooo...." Suddenly, he grabbed his head, and his body slumped to the ground. He lay there still, very still.

What do I do now? My gaze froze on an object nearby. Directly in front of me was a white bucket, half hidden by the weeds. Clasped to the wire handle, close to where it attached to the bucket's rim, was a gleaming trinket in the shape of a lion's head.

In that moment, it all clicked. *He's the window washer...he's the murderer.* I had been closer to the truth in the hallway than I knew. Now I was too close. I looked down at the ropes crisscrossing my chest. Even if I could reach all of them, I didn't have a clue how to untie the complex knots.

Rubbing the back left pocket of my jeans against the headstone, I could feel the flashlight press into my back. *Could I push it up and out of my pocket?* I wiggled and pressed repeatedly until I could feel it rising. After a few minutes, the flashlight dropped to the granite base. I threw my leg to the side to keep it from rolling to the ground. I leaned over, reaching out. The rope grazed my neck. *Lean more.* My right arm couldn't reach any further. I tried to stretch my left arm. My left hand made contact with the cold surface. Carefully, I felt around until, finally, my fingers closed around the flashlight.

I had to remind myself to breathe. My chest felt heavy. *How long have I been here?* I twisted my arm. My watch said 4:26. *Four more minutes and the bus will pass by.*

I looked at the crumpled figure of the murderer. *What if he wakes up? What can I fight with?* My feet and legs were free, but they felt cold and stiff. *I could kick him in the crotch.* That might slow him down, but it wouldn't stop him.

Get a grip. Take inventory. I grimaced. Bracing my hands on my thighs, I forced my head to turn to the right. *No. Don't look at her.* Avoiding the face of Necrodite, the ugly stepsister of Aphrodite, I scanned her body for potential weapons. She, too, had a chest harness of ropes that pressed her body tightly to the headstone. She seemed dressed for a party. Her sleeves were a silky red, her pants, black satin, and she wore a wide, red leather belt around her small waist. *Nothing I could use* Then I looked at her feet. She was wearing close-toed mules in mock-alligator leather, with wooden soles and three-inch square heels! Her legs were crossed at the knee. *The shoes!*

I swung my right leg her way, hooking the toe of my hiking boot underneath the heel of the slide. The shoe slipped off easily enough, but it was tricky to get it hooked over the toe of my boot. I raised it up to clear the weeds. The shoe dangled precariously. *Careful now. Go slow.* I rotated my leg, bending at the knee, being careful to keep the shoe balanced as I brought my foot closer to my right hand. It teetered. And then I grabbed it. I blew out the air from my cheeks. Whew! *Plan B in place.*

What Plan B? Hit him over the head with this shoe? It struck me as a lame idea. What chance would I have wielding a pump against a baseball bat?

4:28. I clutched the shoe tighter in my right hand. *It's time.* With my left hand, I clicked on the flashlight. The halogen bulbs threw out a long, pie-shaped beam of light through the weeds, just as the sun dropped out of sight.

I kept my eyes on the man's form as I lifted the flashlight, directing the light toward the road. Think of a song. *The wheels on the bus go round and round, round and round, round and round, the wheels on the bus go round and round, all the way home.* I concentrated on the tune as I flipped the switch on and off to the beat of the music. *Come on, bus driver.* Flip, flip, flip. I sent up a prayer: *Save me.*

Chapter 29: Death Watch

Minutes ticked by like days. Finally, at exactly 4:31, my ears picked up the sound of an engine approaching. *Yes, God!* The lights of the number 5 Dorseyville – Aspinwall bus broke through the pines. *Finally!* I aimed my flashlight signal directly at the bald-headed driver. Flip, flip, flip.

At the same time, I sent out mental messages to him: *Please stop! Help me, help me, help me!*

The sound of brakes grinding to a stop in the loose gravel never came. The bus roared on by. The loud engine noise faded to a hum and disappeared into the distant murmurs of approaching night. I turned off the light to save the batteries in case another car should appear.

Tears streamed down my face. *Who am I kidding? No other cars will appear. Not all the way out here. I'm lost, cold, tired, hungry, scared—deathly scared.* I was alone with a monster and his latest prize. I almost felt her spirit sympathizing with me. *Had she been in my place before? Had it once been her turn to hope against hope?* I couldn't even bear to look at her.

I thought of my family. Imagining their faces made me quiver, moving me closer to a breakdown. I couldn't think of them now.

Instead, I looked at the shoe in my hand. Even that made me cry. *I'm not old enough to wear a shoe like this. I've never been to a formal dance. Maybe Art would have asked me to the prom next year.*

More tears flooded my eyes. *Art. He'll never forgive me for this. He'll wonder how I could have been so stupid. Will he miss me?* My nose ran. *I'll miss him.*

And Fawn. Oh, Fawn, I'm so sorry. You have always been the wise one. I should have listened to you. I should never have come here. I was drooling now. As I sniffled, something in the weeds moved.

Chapter 30: A Race Against Time

The monster shook his head. He tried to stand, fell back, and tried again. It was completely dark now. I wondered if his eyes were accustomed to the darkness, if he could see me as well as I could see him. I tucked the shoe under my leg but kept my hand grasped tightly around it.

"Waiting for someone?" he asked in a raspy voice. He was standing now.

I shook with the cold of every body in this place.

"You were going to untie me before you fell asleep," I said through chattering teeth.

He laughed. "You aren't a very good actress."

"How did you know I'd be here?"

"I heard you and your friend talking. You said you were look-ing for the third body." He swung his arm wide and pointed to Necrodite. "Well, *there* she *is!*"

He bent down, feeling the ground for the baseball bat. I knew he had found when I heard it clang against the bucket.

I saw him rise again. *This is it. Will it hurt?*

"Did you and Mr. Sanguine kill those women?" I asked.

"Who? That crazy artist? I've never even met him."

"You killed them by yourself?"

"I did."

"Why?"

"*Why?* Because they're all no-good actresses, like my wife. Got a taste of the theatre and wanted to run off with the leading man. And she lied. Right up to the night she was planning to leave, nothing but lies. Lying, cheating tramp!"

I sensed his anger building, spreading through his body like a nuclear reaction. I knew he was gonna hit me.

I grabbed the flashlight and flipped the switch. The beam of light hit him straight in his eyes.

He reached up to shield them with one hand, raising the bat with the other.

Just like baseball except, this time, keep your eye on the bat. He swung the bat above his head, then straight down. I leaned to the side and felt the rope cut into my neck. At the moment of impact, the bat hit the headstone with an ear-splitting crack. The blow caused him to lose his balance. The force of the swing carried his body forward. He tripped, falling directly toward me. I raised my arm with the shoe and struck his head with the square-cut heel as hard as I could.

His body slumped in my lap as I screamed for all I was worth.

I don't know how many minutes passed before I realized no one could hear me. I could feel the wet spot beneath his head spreading over my pants. I wanted to grab him by the hair, as gross as that seemed, and throw him off my lap.

Is he dead? I can't hear him breathing. What if he isn't dead? I could only hear the pounding of my heart in my chest. I felt like I was drowning. *Did I kill him? Oh, I couldn't have killed a person. I didn't mean it; it was self-defense. If he isn't dead, will this psycho wake up and kill me?*

I was desperate to scream again. Who would rescue me? *Fawn, she knows I'm here!* I wanted to shine the flashlight on my watch to see what time it was, but I didn't dare risk waking the man who held me captive, if he was alive. The artist's reception must be over by now. Fawn must be wondering what happened to me. I mentally screamed out to her, *I'm here, Fawn! Help me! Tell someone where I am!*

I ached all over. Exhausted from cold and fear, I leaned my head back against the freezing rock and closed my eyes. *Please, God, forgive me for killing someone. If You'll get me out of this, I'll be a much better person, I promise. I'll never tell an-*

other lie again. I swear. If my mother didn't love me and want me around, I knew God did. After all, He understood the dreadful case of willfulness with which I had been born.

I thought about my room at home. I could see the bookshelves next to my bed filled with all of my books I had kept since I was little. Those books had saved me then. When things got tough with my mom, reading took me to other worlds where I was safe, and brave, and loved. I kept my mind focused on remembering, revisiting those worlds where I had traveled long ago.

Chapter 31: The Game is Up

Mr. Sanguine stood quietly, assessing his self-portrait that was prominently displayed in the middle of the room. The eyes in the painting seemed to follow the guests as they moved about the room.

Yes, it carries well from a distance. Good value contrast. The dark, somber tones couldn't have been done better by Rembrandt himself. But how old and sad that man in the painting looks…do I look like that? Funny, how the eyes can see what the heart cannot.

A commotion behind him interrupted his thoughts. Annoyed, he turned. The crowd was parting. People pushed back on both sides, finding new spaces to occupy, stepping on toes.

A police officer directed the crowd back with his hands, as another approached through the newly created aisle.

134

"Mr. Sanguine?" the first officer asked.

He nodded.

"You're under arrest for the murders of Atalia Trinski and Marie Anna Gephardt."

"*Who?*"

"The two women you murdered. Their personal property is depicted in your paintings right here in this room."

"*What?*" Mr. Sanguine raised both hands and clasped his hair. His eyes drifted from one person to another, as if beseeching them to connect with him, human to human.

But no one returned his gaze. Instead, they looked away.

A thin, well-dressed boy stepped forward and tugged on the officer's sleeve. "*Wait!*" The single word was spoken in a voice barely above a whisper.

The crowd hushed.

"I don't think he's the murderer," the boy said softly.

"Tucker Riggoli? Aren't you one of the kids who found Atalia Trinski's body?"

He nodded.

Another boy and a girl emerged from the crowd. The three teens then proceeded to explain to the crowd how they had recognized the clues in the paintings and notified the police.

Mr. Sanguine slumped to the floor, placing his head in his hands. "I'm not a murderer!" he cried. "I didn't kill anybody!"

Tucker Riggoli cleared his throat and spoke in a whisper, "I think he's innocent."

The officers listened intently as the quiet boy spoke intelligently, with sound logic, explaining how he had arrived at his conclusion.

With tears in her eyes, the girl said urgently, "Officer, I think my friend, Priscilla Griggs, is in danger."

"*Priggs?*" The artist leapt to his feet. Lights flashed in his eyes. "*Where is she?*"

The girl continued, "She went to Crestwood Cemetery to look for a third body. She was supposed to be back by now. If Mr. Sanguine isn't the murderer...."

Her voice trailed off as the officer grabbed his cell phone.

Chapter 32: Help!

"PRIGGS!"

I snapped my head forward. *"Here!"* I screamed, fumbling for the flashlight. I flipped the switch and pointed the light toward the sky, moving it in circles like a beacon.

Hearing voices, I dropped the beam of light down across the weeds to help them find their way to me.

Two policemen ran forward with guns drawn. One grabbed the murderer and yanked him off of me. The limp window washer's body tumbled to the ground. The officer bent down to put hand-cuffs on him. Another officer pulled out a knife and cut away the ropes that held me.

"I think I killed him!" I cried. "And he killed that woman." Shakily, I motioned toward her without turning my head.

The man in blue bent over him. "No, he's breathing. And she's alive, too."

Did I hear him right? "Alive?"

He nodded. "She received a nasty blow to the head, but she still has a pulse." He turned to the other officer. "Is that ambulance close by?"

"It's pulling up now," he responded.

"Young lady, you may have saved her life."

"I think she saved mine." For the first time, I looked hard at her upper body. Her chest was moving ever so slightly. If I hadn't been so afraid, I might have realized she wasn't dead. How long had she been tied to that icy headstone? Her skin was awfully cold. *God, please let her survive.*

"Oh, Priggs!" Fawn's voice cut through the night.

Fawn, Art, Tucker, and Mr. Riggoli were running toward me. Flashlights bounced light around like floodlights in a theater. Fawn took one look at the crusty blood on the woman's face and fainted. Mr. Riggoli caught her as she fell, patting her face with his hand.

"Thank you," was all I could manage to say.

"Thank Fawn," Art said. "She told us where you were. And thank Tucker. He figured out that Mr. Sanguine wasn't the murderer. And thank God we found you!" He looked over at the window washer. "Is he…the murderer? Did you conk him on the head?"

Wiping tears from my eyes, I nodded.

He shook his head, then smiled at me. "*Amazing.*"

138

Chapter 33: Healing

The lights would forever flood my memory of that night—the lights atop the police cars circling the cemetery like beams from a lighthouse, the red ambulance lights flashing in my face, and the stark, cold, white, fluorescent lights of the hospital waiting room. They were in sharp contrast to the feeling of sudden darkness I experienced when my mother walked into the Emergency Room reception area.

"Of all the...Priggs, *what* did *you* do? This is the *biggest* mess you've *ever* gotten yourself into. But *why* should I be surprised? If your father were home, he would deal with you. But no, it's always up to me."

Art clenched his fists, but it was Mr. Riggoli who raised his hand to her, putting his arm around her shoulders, so small compared to his.

139

"Mrs. Griggs," he said, "you've had a bad shock. Why don't you sit down? You must be feeling awful."

My mother looked at him, bewildered.

"Yes, if this had happened to my son, I would have been worried sick. I couldn't imagine Tucker in any danger. What would I do without him? That's how you feel, too, isn't it? But Priggs is okay—she only received some scratches. Can I get you a cup of water?"

My mother nodded, stunned into silence.

When Mr. Riggoli came back with the filled paper cup, handed it to her, and spoke gently, "She's your own precious child, your baby. You want to protect her. I can understand how you feel."

He seemed to have a calming effect on my mother. She got up and walked over to me.

I didn't know whether I should cower or not. I reached a hand up to touch the rope burn on my neck, just in case I would have to ward off a blow.

My mother didn't hit me, however. Instead, she reached down and wrapped her arms around me. "I'm sorry," she whispered in my ear.

For the first time in many years, I felt tears in my eyes as I rubbed my cheek against her plain, navy cotton sweater. I pressed my face into the softness of her chest and inhaled a scent I always associated with Mom—the sweet, clean smell of baby powder. Then I realized the others were watching us. I released her quickly. Mom walked back and sat down quietly next to Mr. Riggoli.

I noticed Tucker sitting on the other side of of his father, smiling broadly. I had never seen him look so happy.

"How did you know Mr. Sanguine wasn't the murderer, Tucker?" I asked.

"Oh, it was easy," he said in a surprisingly rich, strong voice. "At first I wondered why an artist would kill a woman just to paint her shoes. It didn't seem to be enought of a motive. Then there was something my dad said."

Mr. Riggoli looked at his son intently.

"You said that since these were such violent muders, the murderer must hate women."

His dad nodded. "That was the police investigator's theory."

"But Mr. Sanguine painted the women to look beautiful. Priggs wasn't sure he was guilty, either, or she wouldn't have left the reception to look for another body. Finally, I saw the artist's reaction when he was arrested. What motive would he have to murder those women? I just knew he didn't do it."

"Good deductions, son," Mr. Riggoli said proudly. He turned to me, "I overheard the nurse say that the woman you saved is expected to make a complete recovery, thanks to you."

My mother raised her eyes in surprise.

"Mrs. Griggs, your daughter did a very good thing for our community." He gave her a reassuring smile. "How about you and I go finish up the paperwork so we can get these kids home?" He turned to us. "We'll be right back."

They walked over to the front desk.

Just then, Mr. Sanguine rushed through the automatic door. I waved and he ran over to me. He reached out and grasped both of my hands in his as he studied my dirty face, the marks on my neck, and the blood stains on my pants. "Priggs, are you all right?"

"I am now," I said.

"Are you sure?" He leaned in to get a better look at my neck.

"Yes, the doctor checked me out. It's been an awful night."

"It certainly has! I just finished giving the police officer my statement when they brought the window washer in. I came here as quickly as I could."

"I'm really sorry we had you arrested," Art said.

"You thought *I* was a murderer?"

"The red shoes, the purse, and the earrings were all in your paintings—items that belonged to the dead women," Fawn said. "What else could we think?"

Art looked closely at Mr. Sanguine. "Who but the murderer could have seen them?"

"I saw them," Mr. Sanguine replied, "but not on any murder victims. The women were in the apartment across from mine. That's where the window washer lives. I think he brought the women home with him."

He ran his fingers through his hair. "I admit to being strange. I can't paint at night because the light isn't good. Instead, I sometimes look out the window. As an artist, it's my job to observe life. Those floor-to-ceiling windows reveal a lot. Sometimes I look through my binoculars. Usually, there's nothing interesting to see but, one night, I noticed a woman in that apartment wearing beautiful red shoes." He looked at me. "It was her shoes that inspired the painting."

"But why did you paint Mrs. Glassport wearing them?" I asked.

"Because the woman I saw in the window didn't sit still long enough for me to capture her likeness."

"Did you see the window washer murder the women?" Tucker asked.

"Oh, no! The women were most definitely alive—at least they were before he closed the blinds."

Another question occurred to me. "Why didn't you call the police when you saw the news report about the murders on TV?"

"TV? I don't own a TV. That's a pastime for boring people."

I didn't comment on how only a bored person would spy on other people through binoculars.

"Why did you say 'a model to kill for'?" Fawn asked.

"What? How did you hear that?" he asked, his old bluster returning.

I winced. "I heard you say it when I came to spy on you. I was hiding in the hallway around the corner."

"*You—spying on me?*" The artist's voice boomed, then dropped back to a normal tone, "I meant *you* when I said a model to kill for. I knew you were spying on me. I saw you when the wind blew the door open. I watched you in my hand mirror." Now it was his turn to look sheepish. "You see, it's been a long time since I had a pretty, young model to sit for me. I was thrilled to paint you when you came to my studio for lessons." He laughed. "I guess we're even. We're not as honest as we look, are we, Priggs?"

"Looks *can* be deceiving," I said quietly, more to myself than anyone. I turned to Art. "I had a feeling Mr. Sanguine might not be the murderer when I saw the paintings in his closet."

"I told you to stay out of my closet!" the artist bellowed.

I bowed my head. "I wanted to see if the third dead woman was in there, but she wasn't. There were only paintings—and all of them were of the same woman."

"That's my Lily," Mr. Sanguine said in a voice that sounded far away. "She was my sweetheart, my model, my muse. She loved beautiful clothing, jewelry, anything that sparkled, and I loved painting her. But we didn't always get along. I guess you kids are too young to understand about lovers' quarrels."

I didn't look at Art's face.

"One day she left me. Said I was too difficult to live with, too wrapped up in my work. She said I had withdrawn from life."

"Maybe she was right," I said, but immediately wished I hadn't.

He looked up, surprised. "Well, perhaps I am too reclusive. Maybe I need to get out more, get to know more people in this town. Maybe I could show them this." He smiled as he pulled a card out of his pocket.

We gathered around to see what it said.

"Phipps & Cranston Fine Art Gallery," I read aloud. "In New York?" I looked up at Mr. Sanguine. "Is this your big break?"

"It is!" Mr. Sanguine's face glowed from an inner light.

"Does this mean you'll be moving there?" Fawn asked.

"No. I belong here in Aspinwall; this is my home. I'll send my work to their gallery and, once in awhile I'll make a trip to New York to attend shows and receptions." He noticed my look of relief. "I hope you'll come back for more art lessons, Priggs, and maybe you'll sit for me again."

I didn't even have to think about it. "Definitely!"

"Well, that solves the mystery," Fawn said.

"Not quite," said Tucker. "Why did the window washer kill those women?"

"He was deranged," I explained. "He talked to me like I was an actress and kept saying that he knew I was cheating on him. He said his wife was an actress who ran away with her leading man."

"What was the window washer's name?" Fawn asked.

Mr. Sanguine answered. "It was painted on his van: Nimm's Window Washing Service." And Nimms was the last name of the woman on the cover of *Playhouse Digest* he dropped outside of my studio. Amanda Nimms. Maybe she was his wife."

"But how did he find the actresses and get them to go home with me?" I asked.

Tucker offered a partial answer, "My dad said he worked as a part-time actor at the Benedom Theatre."

"Maybe that's how he met those women. Maybe they willingly agreed to enter his apartment," Art said, "but how did he get them out of the building after he killed them without making noise? How could he get them down the stairs and out the front door without being seen?"

Mr. Sanguine smiled. "He probably used the freight elevator at the back of the building. The maintenance people have a key. He could have parked his van right beside the elevator door."

"So that's how he did it," Fawn said. "I'm glad it's over now and you're safe, Priggs." She hugged me to her. "What would I ever do without you?"

"What would I do without you?*"* I asked her back, squeezing her tightly. I was awfully glad neither one of us would ever have to find the answer to that question.

Chapter 34: What Will Be, Will Be

The next day, Art, Tucker, and I went over to Fawn's house, where we repeated the whole story for her parents. Responding with gasps of fear and disbelief, they relived the nightmare with us, sighing with relief at the end. Afterwards, we feasted on homemade rigatoni and Hungarian goulash, garlic bread and warm potato salad, spumoni ice cream and baklava, a strange combination dinner from two parents who loved Fawn more than anything.

Wiping his mouth on his napkin, Art cleared his throat. "Tarpinski said we got an A+ for our report on Captain Bridgeway. He said the extra credit work pushed it from good to exceptional. Any of you know what he was talking about?"

147

Fawn lowered her head, smiling behind a waterfall of hair.

Tucker shook his head.

I softly bit my lower lip. "I can't say. But I guess that means you and Tucker are now a step closer to those dream colleges." Tucker and Art would have to find out about Olivia Lindsey on their own. "And Fawn," I said, "maybe you can collect the $50 reward for an 'A' your parents have been promising you for years."

Mr. and Mrs. Flodi laughed and nodded.

Before I knew it, it was time to go.

Tucker called his mom for a ride, even though he could have walked.

"Wanna walk me halfway home, Fawn?" I asked. We always walked each other halfway.

"Oh, Priggs, I would, but Mr. Tarpinski will kill me if I don't have my history homework done tomorrow. I should do it now."

"That's okay," I said, not wanting to quench her new thirst for knowledge. *Who knew where this might lead?* "I can walk by myself."

"Come on," Art said, "I'll walk you home."

We meandered out into the starlit night as if we were just an ordinary couple going for a stroll on an unusually warm, winter evening.

"So, Miss Dorseyville, what sign are you? Let's see...April...isn't that the sign of the firecracker?"

I laughed. "There is no sign of the firecracker!"

"I'll bet there was the night you were born."

We walked a little way in silence.

"So where will you be five years from now?" he asked. "No, let me guess. You'll get out of this hick town and go off to a big city—Chicago…New York…no, Hollywood."

"What about you? Are you gonna leave this place?" I asked.

"Yes. I'm going to law school. I plan on becoming a rich lawyer with lots of girlfriends."

"Oh, get out!"

"What about me? What will I be?" I tugged on his arm.

"You, Priggs," he stopped walking and looked at me, "you'll be famous."

I looked at him. I couldn't tell if he was kidding or not. "Do you really think so?"

"I know so. I've known it since you were five. It's the only thing you ever wanted, and you will be, someday."

I felt off-balance. Art had never said anything so nice to me.

"And you'll forget about me," he said.

"Oh, if only I could." I jabbed his ribs, trying to get us back on our old, familiar ground.

"But maybe you'll remember the night when this tall, handsome guy walked you home."

"Pini, you're not as tall as you're gonna be."

"Ohhhh…so that's how you want it. Do you think you could stop calling me 'Pini'?"

"Okay…Art."

"I don't suppose you'd like me to call you Priscilla?"

"No way! And don't you ever call me Prissy!"

He laughed. "I won't. What's your middle name?

"Anne, with an 'e'."

"May I call you Anne?"

It rolled off his tongue with ease, like Anne of Green Gables...Anne Frank...or Ann of a Throusand Days. Something stirred in the air around us like the swirling wings of a zillion invisible hummingbirds.

Perhaps he mistook my silence for disapproval because he tried again. "How about Annie?"

I nodded and bit my lip, trying not to show how happy I felt.

"Well, Annie, you aren't as much woman as you're gonna be, but you're more woman now than you think you are—more than any girl I know. I like you just the way you are. What do you think of that?"

It might have been him who moved forward first, or it might have been me. We met in the middle. The next thing I knew, he was kissing me, with lips as soft and warm as toasted marshmallows. He smelled sweet and spicy, like hot chocolate and autumn leaves. And he kissed like...well, some things I can't describe. If heaven is dished out in slices on rare days, like on your birthday, that was one delicious slice.

I don't remember what followed the kiss. I don't remember if we walked on or if we teased each other or if we argued. But he was right about one thing. I would never forget the night that tall, handsome guy walked me home.

Author's Note

The story of Andrew and Alexander Bridgeway (also known as Olivia Lindsey) is fiction based on fact.

As many as 400 women posed as men, enlisted, and served in the ranks during the Civil War. My account of Olivia Lindsey is based one of them, Jennie Hodges, who served with the 95th Illinois Infantry Volunteers as Albert Cashier.

Jennie made it through the whole war without her gender being discovered. How was this possible? During the mandatory physical examination, soldiers would often be asked, "You have pretty good health, don't you?" All they had to show were their hands and feet.

She continued to pose as a man until 1911, when an automobile struck her. That's when the attending physician discovered the truth. Jennie/Albert pleaded with the doctor to keep her secret, and the doctor decided there was no reason her sexual identity needed to become public knowledge.

The stories of Jennie Hodge's early days are varied and conflicting, as are many facets of her incongruous life. By far the most romantic reason for her chosen lifestyle is the one she gave to the nurse who attended her after her automobile accident: Jennie said she had assumed a male name and dress because she was in love.

She and her lover had enlisted at the same time to be together, but he had been wounded and died in the war. Before his death, he had asked Jennie to promise that she would never let another man see her in woman's dress. And she never did.

Jennie Hodges/Albert Cashier is buried at Sunnyslope Cemetery, Saunemin, Illinois. On Memorial Day, 1977, the people of Saunemin, who never forgot their little soldier of the Civil War, erected a new and larger monument to mark the burial site. It reads:

Albert D. J. Cashier
Co. G. 95. Inf.
Civil War
Born: Jennie Hodges
in Clogher Head, Ireland
1843 – 1915

Because I could not find a Civil War veteran buried in Dorseyville or Aspinwall, Pennsylvania, I invented Olivia Lindsey/ Alexander Bridgeway based upon the story of Jennie Hodges. It seemed to me that Priggs might have been a bit like Jennie, had she lived in that era.

Art, Tucker, and Fawn are based on very real people—my childhood friends. And that kiss between Art and Priggs—did that really happen? Many years ago, I made a promise to a tall, handsome guy that I would never tell.

About the Author

Jeanne Lazo grew up in Cheswick, Pennsylvania, not far from Dorseyville and Apsinwall, the setting for IF LOOKS COULD KILL. "As kids, my two older sisters, friends, and I were allowed to roam freely in the woods around our homes," said Jeanne. "I spent a lot of time climbing trees; eating picnic lunches on top of a giant rock; hiking along dirt trails; jumping across streams; sledding and ice skating in winter; biking and swimming in summer; and building forts, tree houses, and wishing wells in all seasons. The land had a tremendous influence on me, as did the sense of freedom it provided to girls as well as boys."

From the time Jeanne learned to read, she was rarely without a book, and every book she read sparked an adventure in her mind. She would act out these adventures on a secret stage atop a fallen tree. Often, she re-enacted movie stories with neighborhood friends, complete with costumes supplied by her friend's mother.

She loved all types of art, including drawing and painting, creating things from paper or items found in the woods, building homes for animals, and sewing doll clothes. "I don't think I ever completely grew up," she said. "I still love those things!"

Over the years, Jeanne helped companies solve problems, wrote reports, managed people, taught college math classes, tutored high school students, and raised a family. When all of that was finished, she mentally traveled back to those imaginary places, wrote her stories, and became a published author.

Today, Jeanne lives with her husband, Gene, in Southern California, along with chickens, turkeys, a cat, and a dog.

How to Write Kids' Mysteries
A Guide for Teen and Adult Writers
A Companion to If Looks Could Kill

by Jeanne Lazo

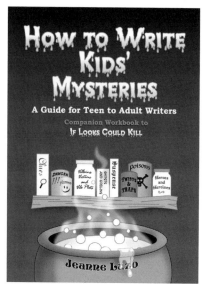

Is there a kids' mystery inside of you dying to get out? Whether you're a teen or adult writer, this amazingly creative workbook is for you!

Short, easy-to-read, sound-bite lessons will help you begin writing your mystery immediately. You don't have to be an "A" student, a genius-born writer, or in the top 10% of your class. You do need to have a burning desire to write the most puzzling, frightening, or challenging story you can...a story kids can't wait to eat up...the most fun story in the universe—a mystery!

Learn from the pros how to:

- Plan a Mystery—the Easy Way
- Create Characters Kids Will Love
- Write Scenes and Settings That Come Alive
- Sprinkle Clues
- Use a Suspense Ladder to Build Blockbuster Tension
- Listen for Rhythm
- Add Creative Icing to Your Mystery
- Design Fabulous Page Layouts

Exercises, examples, and ideas add spice to each sound-bite lesson. You'll love the *Writer's Toolkit*, which includes handy tools, such as alternative words to 'said', words to avoid, words for the five senses, words for movements, and more. This is a must-have resource for beginning to advanced writers; creative writing teachers in middle schools, high schools, colleges, or adult education classes; school and public libraries; and writing clubs.

Ages Teen to Adult   144 pages   8½" x 11"   See Website for Price
ISBN: 1-933277-00-9   Softcover

STARGAZER
Publishing Company
PO Box 77002
Corona, CA 92877-0100

www.stargazerpub.com

The Phantom Hunters!™
NEW ADVENTURE/MYSTERY SERIES!
Book #1: The Lost Treasure of the Golden Sun
by Carol J. Amato

Although 12-year-old Anny and Scout Bradford are identical twins, the resemblance ends with their blond hair and blue eyes. Scout is outdoorsy, good at all things athletic, and a dedicated Girl Scout. Anny is different, very different. She sees things other people don't. Most grownups think she's crazy or lying—even her own family. Everyone, including Anny, wonders what's wrong with her.

When Anny sees a startling vision of a warrior on a trip to the Navajo Nation, once again, no one believes her—no one except her close friend, Eric Larson. He knows what it's like to be misunderstood. He's deaf.

Anny senses her vision has something to do with lost treasure, a mysterious fire, and two visiting archaeologists. She and Eric set out to convince Scout and their friend, Ben Lapahie, that the mysterious warrior is real. But is he good or evil? Is he leading them to the answers to the location of the treasure and who set the fire or to an untimely end?

Ages 10 and Up   184 pages   5½" x 8½"   See Website for Price
Hardcover, English   ISBN: 1-933277-01-7
Softcover, English   ISBN: 0-9713756-5-8
Softcover, Spanish   ISBN: 0-9713756-3-1

STARGAZER
Publishing Company
PO Box 77002
Corona, CA 92877-0100

www.phantomhunters.com

If Looks Could Kill
Teacher's Guide

by Jeanne Lazo

If Looks Could Kill, a middle-grade mystery for girls and boys, provides classroom tie-ins to mystery writing and analysis, Civil War history, women in history, child abuse, reasoning, and logic.

Teachers will love this accompanying Teacher's Guide packed with innovative tools to stimulate classroom discussions that will get every child actively involved. Exercises and activities are cross-referenced to California Department of Education Standards and correlate to the curriculum in:

- History
- Visual Arts
- Social Studies
- Research and Technology
- Mystery Genre Analysis
- Language Conventions
- Narrative Writing
- Descriptive Strategies
- Reading Comprehension
- Geography

Grades 6-8   32 pages   8½" x 11"   See Website for Price
ISBN: 1-933277-05-X Softcover

STARGAZER
Publishing Company
PO Box 77002
Corona, CA 92877-0100

www.stargazerpub.com